The
Private
Lives
of
Pippa
Lee

Rebecca Miller

CANONGATE
Edinburgh · London

This Canons edition published by Canongate Books in 2016

First published in Great Britain in 2008 by Canongate Books Ltd,
14 High Street, Edinburgh EH1 1TE

www.canongate.tv

Published in the United States in 2008 by Farrar, Straus & Giroux,
18 West 18th Street, New York, NY 10001

1

British Library Cataloguing-in-Publication Data
A catalogue record for this book is available on
request from the British Library

Every efforthas been made to trace copyright holders and to obtain
their permission for the use of copyright material.
The publisher apologises for any errors or omissions and would be
grateful if notified of any corrections that should be incorporated in
future reprints or editions of this book.

Typeset by Palimpsest Book Production Limited,
Falkirk, Stirlingshire

Printed and bound in Great Britain by Clays Ltd, St Ives plc

ISBN 978 1 78211 915 9

To D.

– And for Barbara Browning

Part One

Part One

Wrinkle Village

Pippa had to admit, she liked the house.

This was one of the newer units, they were told. Dishwasher, washing machine, dryer, microwave, electric oven, all new. Carpeting, new. Septic tank. Roof. Yet the floor of the basement had a crack in the concrete, and some of the grouting between the tiles in the bathroom was turning dark with mold. Signs of decay, like in an old mouth with gleaming caps glued over the stumps, Pippa thought. She wondered how many people had died in this house. Marigold Village, retirement community: a prelude to heaven. This place had everything: swimming pool, restaurants, mini-mall, gas station, health food store, yoga classes, tennis courts, nursing staff. There was an on-call grief counselor, two marriage counselors, a sex therapist, and an herbalist. Book club, camera club, garden club, model boatbuilding club. You never had to leave. Pippa and Herb had first encountered Marigold Village when returning to their Long Island beach house from a lunch party in Connecticut twenty years earlier, when Pippa was just past thirty, Herb sixty. Herb had taken a wrong turn, and they found themselves on a narrow, winding road lined with clusters of dun-colored, single-story houses. It was five o'clock in April; the late afternoon light cast a golden filter over the perfectly maintained lawns. The houses looked identical; a hive of numbered mailboxes stood at the end of each shared driveway. Some of the numbers were in the thousands. Herb had been confident that a couple of left turns and a right would put them back on the main road, but every turn he made seemed to suck them deeper into the development.

'It's like one of those fairy tales,' Pippa said.

'What fairy tales?' Herb asked, exasperation in his voice. Pippa was always seeing poetry in everything. Leave it to her to turn getting lost in a housing development into something out of the Brothers Grimm.

'You know,' she said, 'where the children enter the forest, and everything shifts, all the landmarks magically change, and they get lost, and then there's usually a witch of some kind.' The trees rose to hide the last of the sun. The light went dull.

'At least a witch could give us directions,' Herb grumbled, turning the steering wheel. His massive hands made it look like a toy.

'I think we passed that fountain before,' she said, looking back.

A futile twenty minutes later, they found themselves at the Marigold gas station. A friendly teen in a navy blue uniform showed them the way out. It was so simple: two rights and a left. Herb couldn't believe he hadn't figured it out. Days later, when they heard Marigold Village was a retirement community, they laughed. Wrinkle Village, it was called by the locals. 'We were lost for so long,' Herb would say when telling the story, 'we almost had to retire there.'

That story got the biggest laugh yet at the housewarming party Pippa threw on their third Saturday in Marigold Village. Many of their dearest friends were there to quizzically usher in their new life in the development.

Sam Shapiro, an angular, balding man in his fifties, was probably the finest fiction writer in the country. The massive advance Herb had shelled out for his last novel had made the papers. He stood up and raised his glass to Herb and Pippa, his words firing out of him rapidly, in staggered clusters.

'We all know Herb Lee can be a bastard, but he's usually right. He hates self-pity more than anything, in writing and in life. That makes him a great editor, and a damn tough human being. I can't believe you're eighty, Herb. I guess that means I'm not thirty-five anymore. But I tell you. When it comes to words, Herb's instincts are pitch-perfect. With women, not so much. I think we all know what I'm talking about.' Uneasy laughter rippled through the group, and one man guffawed. Sam continued: 'So when he first told me he was going to marry Pippa, I thought, Here we go again! She seemed like ... radioactive jam. Sweet, but deadly. Herb, however, disregarding my advice, followed his nose, as usual – a significant nose, I might add, not one of these trivial little noses we see all over town these days – and somehow he ended up with the most spectacular woman. I've known Pippa Lee for a quarter of a century, but I'll never really know her. She's a mystery, a cipher, something which is nearly extinct these days: a person not controlled by ambition or greed or a crass need for attention, but by a desire to experience life completely, and to make life a little easier for the people around her. Pippa has nobility. Pippa has style.'

Pippa's lips compressed slightly, her brow furrowed in a private signal of disapproval. She wanted him to glorify Herb, not her. Sam's quick bird's glance rested on her for a moment; reading her signal, he smiled and went on: 'And Herb had the sense to recognize her for what she was, when it was damn hard to tell. So he can't be all bad. I drink to a man who, even at this late stage of his career, remains entirely unpredictable. I can't decide what I think of your choice to move from Gramercy Park to Marigold Village, Herb. If it's humble, or practical, or perverse. But as long as Pippa keeps making that butterflied lamb, I'll even caddie for you, if that's what it comes to.'

'I don't think you'd be much of a caddie, Sam,' said Herb, his mouth creasing into a lopsided grin, as it did whenever he made a crack.

'Never underestimate a hungry Jew!' called out Sam Shapiro.

'I think it's sort of amazing,' said a hurt, adenoidal voice. Moira Dulles was a poet who had been living with Sam for the past few years. She was sitting cross-legged on the floor, at Herb's feet. 'I mean, you left everything behind. Pippa, you are so courageous to just get up and go, start a new life ...'

Pippa watched her fragile friend with concern. She hoped Sam didn't hear the tears in her voice. 'It feels free,' said Pippa. 'No more big households to take care of.'

'Don't wreck my illusions,' said Sam. 'You are the icon of the Artist's Wife: placid, giving, intelligent, beautiful. Great cook. They don't make 'em like that anymore.' Moira Dulles gave him a black look, which he ignored. 'And Herb doesn't even deserve her, he's not an artist. I never thought of that before! The one true artist's wife left in the modern world, and she goes to a publisher!' He cackled, then scraped his breath in with a donkey's bray.

'She wasn't like that when I married her,' said Herb. 'I tamed her.'

'Oh, shut up,' Pippa smiled, drifting into the kitchen and wondering if Sam was teasing Herb too hard. Ben, Pippa and Herb's son, was scouring the roasting tin, glancing up at the party through the hatch that looked out on the dining area. Still in law school, he already had the bad posture and good-natured pessimism of a middle-aged man. He scrutinized his mother through round, professorial glasses.

'I hope Herb is okay,' Pippa said, lighting a small blowtorch and turning it on fifteen pots of crème brûlée. The layer of sugar on each one bubbled and darkened to the color of molasses.

'Mom, he's fine. Nothing could put a dent in his ego.'

'That's what you think.'

'It's you I'm worried about.'

'Oh, I'm fine, sweetheart.'

'Your problem is, you're too adaptable. The adaptable cipher.' Pippa patted Ben's arm. He was always protecting her from harm, whether she wanted him to or not. In the next room, Herb was talking intently to Sam, hunched forward in his chair. He was still so handsome, Pippa thought. Eighty years old with a full head of hair, his own teeth. When was it all going to implode?

'You should do it too,' he was telling Sam. 'If you manage to get old. I recommend it. Turned my whole life into cash. Giving it to them in increments. Otherwise it takes years for the estate to be processed, and then the state takes half.'

'I thought you loved paying taxes!' interjected Don Sexton, a screenwriter whose elongated vowels made him sound like he belonged in *The Philadelphia Story*.

'That's right!' said Phyllis, his sharp-witted wife. 'You always said you wished the government would tax *more*.'

'I'm not funding this fucking war,' Herb said.

'Ah – so it comes down to ethics, after all,' said Sam. 'I was rooting for perversity, myself.'

'Stop boiling it all down,' growled Herb. But he was enjoying being kidded. Pippa suddenly adored Sam Shapiro. He was hitting just the right tone of jocular disrespect with Herb. She had been so worried that people would start to act differently now that the invincible man was in an old people's facility. Treating it like a crazy joke – that was just the thing. The great Herb Lee, heroic owner of one of the last independent publishing houses in the country, virile champion of the Great American Novel – admitting to being old. It seemed unreal to everyone in that room. His frailty made their own middle age palpable. They were up next.

Moving to a retirement community was the last thing Pippa had expected from Herb, but then again, she had learned to accept swift changes in tack from her husband. Beneath Herb's steady-handed, unflappable demeanor lurked a profound impulsiveness; he had bought manuscripts, left publishing houses and even marriages with sudden, lurching decisiveness all his life. Pippa knew that Herb trusted his own instincts deeply, to the point of superstition; perhaps that was all he trusted. Once his internal compass needle moved, that was it – something was going to change. So when he came home, laughing, a pamphlet for Marigold Retirement Village in his fist, saying, 'This is that place we got lost that time!' – then spent the afternoon flipping through the glossy pages in his study, she sensed something was brewing. In the end, he sold the idea to her as a practical solution: 'I've got five, ten years at the most. What do we need the beach house for anymore? The kids are gone. Manhattan is a pain in the ass. We're hemorrhaging money you could use down the line. We liquidate our assets, Pippa, and then when I go, you have most of the money in your pocket. You can travel, buy a small place downtown. If we sell everything, you'll be free.' But Pippa smelled a whiff of fear in this bluster; Herb had had two heart attacks in the space of a week the previous year. For the six subsequent months, she'd had to do everything for him. He couldn't make it up a flight of stairs. Now he napped more than he used to, but he was vigorous again, stronger in some ways, what with his near-perfect diet and all the exercise he was doing, but those excruciating days, when sudden, extreme age was foisted on him and Pippa, had made an indelible mark on their lives. Herb was, Pippa knew, terrified of having her become his nurse. Marigold Village was a sort of preemptive strike against decrepitude, cutting to the chase. It was, in fact, pure Herb: he was unsentimental, realistic, and utterly unwilling to be unmanned.

The fact that Sam Shapiro, who had become Herb's best friend over the past three decades, happened to live fifteen minutes away, was both a boon and a bit of an embarrassment, Pippa knew. Because Sam had followed Herb from one publishing house to another for years before Herb started his own press. Sam had been so loyal to Herb, in fact, that people began to wonder if the great Shapiro needed his editor a little too badly. The air of triumph that Sam exuded upon learning of the move – as if Herb had moved to follow *him* – irritated Herb, even if he *was* just ribbing. In all his relationships, Herb was the master, the desired one. To topple this pyramid would shake the foundations of his personality. Pippa watched Sam carefully for any evidence of a shift in the dynamic of the friendship. She, too, needed Herb to maintain his aura of strength. Tending him in the months after his heart attacks had been confusing. She had loved him perhaps more deeply than ever before, but the shape of their relationship had begun to warp in troubling ways. When they met, he had been her rescuer. For him to be dependent on her embarrassed both of them.

So they sold the house in Sag Harbor with its gray shingles, its cozy rooms layered, decade by decade, with paintings, rugs, objects, photographs. The children's rooms, still cluttered with horse jumping medals and band posters, the expansive master bedroom with its vast bed, the picture window Pippa sat in front of every Sunday, reading the paper or gazing at the birds – the whole of it snapped up one rainy Tuesday by a real estate developer and his wife. The apartment on Gramercy Park went to a couple of childless ophthalmologists. Though Pippa was heartsick to lose these places she had loved, she was surprised to feel released as well. To shed much of what they owned, to be free from superfluity – the impulse had rung out faintly within her for years, like the occasional beep of a cell phone lost deep in an apartment. But it was muffled by the joys, the comforts, the dilemmas of everyday life as a happily married, well-off woman, a dedicated mother, generous hostess, a woman who seemed to those who knew her to be among the most gracious, the kindest, the loveliest, the most unpretentious and most reassuring ladies they had ever met.

Pippa returned to the dining room carrying the tray of crème brûlée. Herb wasn't meant to have so many eggs and so much fat, but she figured that once in a while he should have what he loved, the way he always had, before the doctors caught up with him. Besides, Pippa loved giving pleasure, and every cook knows that lamb and crème brûlée elicit more sighs at the table than flounder and fruit salad. She watched as the guests broke through the little rinks of caramelized sugar with their spoons, bringing the thick, vanilla-scented cream into their mouths.

Cake

Next morning, Pippa was alone in the living room, supine as an odalisque in a turquoise raw silk kimono shirt and jeans. Her rather flat, feline face, with its high cheekbones and almond-shaped, upturned gray eyes, was framed by hair tinted the color of rose gold. Even in middle age, she resembled a Madonna in a Flemish painting, but rounder, juicier. Her head resting on a Moroccan pillow whose geometric pattern was intended to break up the monotony of the taupe Swedish Modern couch she'd bought to go with the clean lines of the condo, she surveyed her living room with satisfaction. Nothing here was extraneous. She had deliberately rescued each vase, bowl, painting from the morass of belongings that the family had built up over the years, most of which she had given to the children or donated to charity with uncharacteristic abandon when they moved to Marigold Village, storing only the few important pieces she thought she or the kids might one day miss. Each object Pippa had selected to survive this merciless culling now seemed charged with memory, isolated as it was from its peers in this sterile backdrop devoid of associations, walls painted dove gray: the luminous red glass ashtray Herb and Pippa bought in Venice on their honeymoon; her mother's treasured heart-shaped candy dish decorated with tiny shamrocks; the conch shell that her children had held up to their ears long ago, transported expressions on their faces, as they listened to the rush of the sea.

This house makes me feel strange, Pippa thought languorously, propping herself up on her elbow and taking a pair of brand-new binoculars from the glass coffee table. The sliding glass doors were open, and Pippa squinted through the powerful lenses at a wall of emerald green lawn with an opal of sparkling blue, a tiny, artificial lake – one of the many that dotted Marigold Village – at its center. She jerked the binoculars back and forth until she spied a bird, an oriole, nervously hopping on a willow branch. The bird had a black hood and saffron yellow chest feathers, fading into white at the abdomen. It looked precisely like the glossy picture of a Baltimore Oriole in Pippa's manual, *Birds of the East Coast*, which she had bought at the Marigold bookstore only a week before.

On the day she purchased the manual, she noticed a sign on the bulletin board in the bookstore: 'Marigold reading group meets every Thursday evening at seven. New members welcome.' This caught her interest. It might be a good way to meet people. The following Thursday, she was knocking on the door of the prescribed unit, wearing one of Herb's shirts and a loose linen skirt. She felt she should hide her still solid body from the old women. It seemed only kind. A tiny lady with the tight white curls and pull-on trousers of the nearly aged swung open the door. 'Another young one!' she pronounced rather loudly, half-looking over her shoulder. 'Come on in. Very exciting, us old crones like new blood.' Pippa introduced herself, walked into the living room, and saw a group of women in their sixties, seventies, and eighties seated in a circle like a witches' coven, purses tucked by their sides; in each of their laps lay a paperback copy of Sam Shapiro's latest novel, *Mr Bernbaum Presents*. Pippa nearly bust out laughing. This was too much.

'I'm Lucy Childers,' said the woman who had answered the door. 'This is, let's see . . . Emily Wasserman, Ethel Cohen, Jean Yelding, Cora O'Hara, and – Where's Chloe?' Just then, the other 'young one' came out from behind the bathroom door. Chloe was of an indeterminate age; her taut face was frozen in a semi-smile, having been ratcheted up several notches and enhanced by prominent cheekbones that looked like Ping-Pong balls under her skin. The two swollen halves of her upper lip drooped suggestively, like a set of red velvet curtains tied at the corners of her mouth, Pippa thought. The tip of her nose was pinched, as though a pair of fingers had squeezed a clay sculpture as a prank. Her eyelids seemed Krazy-Glued open a little too wide. She spoke in a very quiet, level voice, as one might speak to a child having a tantrum.

'It's lovely to meet you,' she said, her startled eyes staring out of that approximation of a face like a prisoner peering out of a chink in a stone wall. Pippa said something polite and looked away, feeling a mix of pity and repulsion.

'This is Chloe's last meeting with the club,' Lucy Childers said. 'Her husband has recently passed and she's moving back to the city.'

'I'm sorry,' said Pippa.

'Thank you,' whispered Chloe.

Lucy Childers perched herself on the edge of the couch, back straight, her small feet in their white leather nurse's shoes lined up beside each other neatly, and opened the discussion with her own erudite thoughts, one tiny, stiff hand chopping the air each time she made a point, then moving it swiftly to the side, as though scraping peelings off a table. Lucy admired the symmetry of the book, the careful pacing, the slow but steady drip feed of information – not too much, not too little; she called it a 'mystery of character.' Then she turned to Chloe, who murmured, 'It's a mean book, but I liked it.' Pippa tried to shrug off the unwelcome mix of dread and kinship she felt with this person.

The oriole flew off. Pippa moved the binoculars down a bit, found Herb's red Converse sneakers. She followed his brown, skinny legs, the little hill of his belly, until she came to his rugged face, lower jaw clamped over front teeth in a grimace of concentration as he read a four-inch-thick manuscript on the lawn chair. The truth was, Herb hadn't retired. He was running the company from here, buying manuscripts, making deals.

A household list filed through Pippa's mind on an endless loop, the way the breaking headlines run under the TV news: *dry cleaning . . . toilet paper . . . plant fertilizer . . . cheese . . .* She had been lying in this luxurious position dreamily for half an hour, having cleaned the house and planned dinner by ten. The circle of the artificial pond, Herb's legs, the brilliant, green lawn . . . Pippa wished she could paint it. It was an odd desire for her; she always said of herself, almost proudly, surrounded as she was by creative folk, that she had no talent of any kind.

The buzz of the doorbell startled her. She sat up and swiveled around to see Dot Nadeau waiting behind the screen door. Dot was a bleach blonde with leathery skin and a sultry, New Jersey voice. She lived just across the artificial lake, in 1272. In their late sixties, Dot and her husband, Johnny, were among the younger residents. Pippa, at fifty, was practically a child bride.

'Do you have a minute?' Dot asked in a muted tone. She looked harried.

'Sure. I'm supposed to be doing errands. But who cares,' said Pippa.

They sat down in the kitchen. Pippa poured out a cup of coffee and handed it to Dot. 'Is everything okay?' she asked.

'Well, we're fine, but . . . my son, Chris. Remember I told you about him?'

'In Utah?'

'Yes. He's thinking of relocating and . . . he might be coming east.'

'Oh, well, that would be nice, if they would move near you.'

'The thing is, he's having trouble . . . It's just a mess, Pippa, a real mess.' There were tears in Dot's eyes. Pippa checked to see that Herb was still ensconced on his lawn chair and fetched Dot a Kleenex.

'What is it?' asked Pippa. She felt awkward. She didn't know Dot very well. They'd had coffee a couple of times, but they'd never gotten past the pleasantry stage.

'He's had some kind of crisis with his wife, and he's left her, and he's lost his job – it wasn't even a real job, he was working in a men's shelter. How do you lose a job like that? I think he's living in his car. Thank God there are no kids. I don't know what to do.'

'Well, he's an adult, I mean . . . what can you do?'

'He was always sort of half-baked, you know what I mean?'

Pippa wondered what Dot meant. Was the boy retarded? A drunk? Stunted in some way?

'It's painful, but sometimes you just have to accept that they are who they are. I mean, I feel that about mine.' Tender Ben and tyrannical Grace. Now and forever. Nothing to be done. As if on cue, Ben walked in pulling a well-worn seersucker jacket over his sloped shoulders. Whenever Pippa saw him, she was amazed he was no longer a boy. 'Hello, darling,' she said. 'Dot, this is my son, Ben.'

'The lawyer!' said Dot, gazing at him admiringly.

'Not yet,' said Ben.

'Columbia, right?' asked Dot. Immediately Pippa felt a pang of guilt for having a son in law school when Dot's boy was unemployed and possibly homeless.

Dot turned to Pippa. 'You're right,' said Dot. 'I knew I should come to you. I had a feeling. I'm just going to let him cry it out on his own. He can't come running to me every time his life falls apart. It's no favor to him.'

'Of course he knows if he's ever really in trouble . . .'

'He has me.' Dot hugged Pippa and left.

Ben bit into an apple. 'What were you right about?'

'I have no idea,' said Pippa. 'She said her son was half-baked, and I said sometimes you have to accept things the way they are.'

'Well, she left satisfied, anyway.'

'Half-baked?' said Herb, who had come in when he heard Ben's voice. 'Is that code for half-wit?'

Pippa took a blood pressure cuff from a drawer, Velcroed it onto Herb's arm, and started pumping it up. Ben stood to read the dial with her.

15

'Since when are you two on the staff of Mount Sinai?' asked Herb. 'Don't get mad,' said Pippa. 'Your blood pressure goes up.'

'How about if I hang myself?' said Herb with a grim smile. 'What happens then?'

'A little appreciation for your ministering angel, Dad,' said Ben in a jocular, warning tone. Herb slid the local paper across the table, scanned the front page, grimacing. He hated having his blood pressure taken in front of people, even the kids. Pippa could feel his petulance rise up in her like a tide. She should have waited till Ben had gone. Shit, she thought. Oh, well. She poured Ben a bowl of Grape-Nuts cereal and listened to the swift animal crunch his teeth made when he ate it, the same crunch they had made when he was five. She loved that sound. 'Oh, by the way,' Ben said. 'Stephanie brought a cat home from the pound.'

'Another one!' she exclaimed, laughing. Ben's girlfriend couldn't resist lame animals. She was a dear, earnest person. Pippa was sure they would produce a fine family, as long as Ben didn't get distracted by someone more exciting. But he didn't seem to crave thrills, strangely enough.

Ben stood up. 'Back to the salt mines,' he said.

'Are you still working on that same paper?' she asked.

He nodded, pushing his glasses back up his nub nose. 'The paper that ate Ben Lee.'

'You're just thorough,' Pippa said.

'I actually think I might be onto something,' he said.

'Isn't that great,' she said, beaming. As she walked him out to his car, he put his arm around her.

'Mom,' he said. 'Come to the city next week and we can have lunch. Or dinner. You can stay over.'

'We're having lunch with Grace on Wednesday.'

'Oh. Right. If you want to get together another time, call me, okay?'

'I will,' she said. 'Of course I will. Stop worrying about me, will you?'

16

'I just want you to have a little fun,' he said.

After Ben drove off, Pippa stood quietly staring after him. The list, which had rolled by under Dot a couple of times while she was talking, came into full view now: *cheese . . . dry cleaning . . . plant fertilizer . . .*

It was only three minutes to the mini-mall. Pippa drove over, picked up all the things she needed at the grocery store, dropped off the dry cleaning, then eased herself back onto the searing car seat and started creeping through the parking lot. She was in terror of mowing over one of the aged people, dressed in pink and pistachio, their tanned faces collapsed, shriveled skin coming away from knees and elbows.

*

The relentless buzzing of a lawn mower dragged Pippa from a black sleep like a body from a river. As she opened her eyes, she felt a dull pain in her temples. She wanted water, and coffee. Sitting up in the bed, she glanced at Herb. As a rule she tried not to look at him when he was sleeping. Eyes shut tight, mouth slack, he looked like an ancient, fragile old man. She turned away and stood. She knew that when his icy blue eyes, with their conquering stare, opened, she would feel reassured again. She loved this man so much. It was a condition she had tried to cure herself of many times; the symptoms could be painful. But she'd given up the fight long ago. She was the woman who loved Herb Lee. Oh, and many other things besides, she thought to herself as she pulled on her cotton robe the color of new leaves. Mother. Two decent, productive human beings living in the world because of me. That's not nothing. She walked into the kitchen, squinting in the blinding light. Everything was white. Formica table, counter, tile floor, lost their edges, bled into a field of light, their perspective flattened. Shadows from the window casings threw a blue grid over the room. With her vision blurred from sleep, the effect was so dazzlingly abstract that she had to take a moment to get her bearings, and when she did she was so confused by what she saw that she questioned her own memory.

The table had been set chaotically, plates scattered at random, as if tossed by a furious domestic. Some of them had chocolate cake on them. Others were bare. Pippa noticed something the color of peanut butter spread on one of the slices of chocolate cake. She sniffed it cautiously. It was peanut butter. Yet she distinctly remembered sponging down the table the night before. The place had been immaculate. A chill went up her spine, and she swiveled around, imagining a malevolent pair of psychotic eyes staring at her from the living room – some escaped lunatic, brandishing a dirty cake knife. Seeing no one, she went to the kitchen door, tried it. Locked. She walked around the house, checked every door, every window. All locked. No one had come in. It must have been Herb. But they had gone to bed together at eleven. Herb had fallen asleep first. She tried to imagine him getting up to let people in, after midnight, for chocolate cake and peanut butter. It was out of the question. Then how had the cake gotten there? She cleared the table, scraped plates into the garbage, and stacked them in the dishwasher. Made coffee.

She was sitting at the table drinking a cup when Herb walked in, opened the front door, and dragged the local paper off the mat.

'So,' she said. 'I can't believe you had a party and didn't invite me.'

'What are you talking about?' he said, putting on his reading glasses.

'You left all the plates out.'

'What plates?'

'Herb, there were six plates with chocolate cake on the table this morning. Or there were six plates. Two of them didn't have any cake on them. One of the slices had peanut butter on it.'

Herb sat and looked at her. 'Have you gone stark raving mad?' he said, laughing.

'At first I thought someone came into the house, but the doors are all locked.' There was a pause as this sank in.

18

'Does anyone else have a key?'

'Well, I guess the maintenance people. And Miss Fanning.'

'The cleaning lady? She lives in New Milford. Why would she drive all the way over here for chocolate cake? We better check if anything is missing.' Nothing was missing. Pippa called Miss Fanning and pretended she was confirming her for Monday. Then she casually asked her what she'd been up to the night before. There was a pause. 'Bowling?' the woman answered tentatively. Herb called the administrative offices to register a complaint. They asked if he wanted to call the police. Herb declined. 'I suppose you could call it a victimless crime,' he said, his nostrils expanding slightly. The man on the other end of the phone chuckled politely.

Pippa called a locksmith, had the locks changed. This time, they gave no one a key. A week went by. Pippa kept thinking about the cake. It had to be Herb. He had forgotten. He was losing his mind. Pippa watched him with special care now. Every time he misplaced his glasses or forgot someone's name, she felt her suspicion grow. Then, the next Sunday morning, she walked into the kitchen and found carrot sticks planted in a bowl of vanilla frosting. A frying pan with the remains of fried ham cemented to the bottom. More dirty plates. This time she woke Herb and showed him. They looked at each other.

'Maybe you should see a doctor,' she said.

Herb was furious. 'Okay, if I have Alzheimer's so be it, I'll kill myself. But first I need to see the evidence.' He drove straight to the electronics store in the mini-mall and bought a small surveillance camera with a wall mount, then paid the man from the store to install it in the corner, where the wall met the ceiling. The guy was up on a ladder, sweat pouring down his face. Pippa turned on the air conditioner. 'This must seem a little strange to you,' she said.

'You'd be surprised what people do for entertainment in this place,' said the man.

'Really?'

'Yeah, but I've never seen it in the kitchen before.'

'Oh. No. It's not – it's –' Pippa let it go. She'd rather have him think they were filming themselves humping on the kitchen table than chronicling her husband's descent into inanity.

An hour later, Pippa was straightening out the living room when she looked out the plate-glass window. Across the pond, in the Nadeaus' driveway, a U-Haul was hitched up to a bright yellow truck with an orange shell clamped over the bed. The shell had windows with ratty blue and red gingham curtains pulled shut inside. Pippa could see Dot gesturing to a dark-haired man who was carrying a cardboard box. Pippa picked her bird-watching binoculars off the coffee table and trained them on the young man. He had a T-shirt with 'What?' printed on the back of it. So the half-baked son was moving in after all! It was funny about Dot, she thought. It felt so natural, talking to her. It made Pippa feel like a different person. Dot knew her out of context. A few months ago, in her old life, she would no sooner have had a friendship with Dot Nadeau than flown around the room. Their friends were editors, novelists, critics, poets. Yet Pippa had never felt fully at ease in their hypercivilized company. Only with her twins, when they were young – only then had she felt fully secure in who she was. Grace and Ben had looked up at her with such certainty in their little faces, and called her Mama. They knew, so she knew. Now her babies were gone. They called sometimes, came home to visit. Occasionally they all went out to lunch together. But they didn't look at Pippa the way they once had. Ben was still so sweet to her. He had always needed little, expected everything, received what he expected. He was born thoughtful, but secure. Pippa's feeling for him was simple, ample, easy. But Grace – that was a real fuckup. Pippa felt stupid and bumbling in her daughter's company, and somehow guilty, as though she had let Grace down by amounting to so little. And there was something more.

As a very young child, Grace had been needy, clutching at her mother like a baby monkey. Her love for Pippa was possessive and competitive. Though she adored her twin, she tried to edge Ben out of her mother's embraces, desperate to bask in her love alone. The day after her fourth birthday she sat down at Pippa's feet, opened a book, and read the whole thing out loud. Pippa was astounded; the child had been completely intractable when it came to reading, refusing to sound out letters at all. Little Grace looked up at her mother then and, with furrowed brow, asked, '*Now* do you love me more than Ben?' Pippa swept the girl up into her lap and hugged her, feeling a sting of guilt like a poisoned needle in her sternum. Because she knew what Grace was getting at. There were flashes of jealous intensity in her daughter's love that Pippa found domineering, devouring, even repellent in moments that came and, mercifully, dissolved again into the otherwise sunny landscape of their daily lives. Once, watching a ship disappear over the lip of the ocean, Grace said to Pippa, 'I own you as far as the eye can see.'

Though she did not recognize it, in some secret part of Pippa's mind, her daughter's wish to possess her utterly echoed another love, a deadly, sweet, and voracious passion that had all but suffocated Pippa in her youth.

Yet, never mind, in spite of it all, now that Grace was grown she was a triumph! So sophisticated, so courageous. Pippa found herself watching her sneakily, out of the corner of her eye. And occasionally, in her daughter's recklessness, her lust for adventure, her desire for experience, she recognized herself, a self that had vanished long ago. How had it happened? How could she have changed so much? She remembered the morning she looked in the mirror and saw three white, bent hairs sticking out of her head. They had looked obscene to her, like stray pubic hairs escaping from the crotch of a bathing suit. Now, beneath the reddish blond tint, her hair was white. Pippa was a placid, middle-aged woman. And Herb was eighty years old. The thought of it made her laugh. Life was getting so unreal.

More and more, the past was flooding into her, diluting the present like water poured into wine.

Herb walked in then. Pippa turned. 'Do you need anything?' she asked.

Herb sat down and patted the pillow beside him. 'How's my pal?' he asked.

'I'm okay,' she said.

'Are you sad that you're living in Wrinkle Village?'

'I have to fill up my days more. But I'm not sad. I think it's sort of romantic, starting again like this, with so little stuff.' Herb smiled sadly and lay back on the cushions. His skin, bronzed from all that time on the patio, was creased like a rock face, his eyes points of light.

'Always looking on the bright side,' he said to her.

'Why can't it be?' There was a pause.

'Maybe we should move back to the city,' he said.

She laughed. 'We just sold our apartment!'

'So we buy another one.'

'Really?'

'No, of course not. It's just hard thinking this is the end of the line.'

Pippa put her hand on his knee and looked around the room. She wondered what she could make for him. Maybe a glass of carrot juice. She had begun to feel a kind of desperation when they were alone sometimes, as if everything that they could possibly say to each other had already been said, and now language was useless.

'That was good cheese yesterday,' Herb said.

'It was vacherin – I was so excited to find it.'

'I love that cheese.'

Another Woman

A week later Pippa woke up with one arm asleep, pinned beneath her side. She felt as though her body had been crushed into the mattress through the night, her face mashed into the pillow. There was a rotten taste in her mouth. She sat up stiffly, shaking the blood back into her numb limb, which flopped helplessly from side to side like a separate being.

In the kitchen, a thick, yellow continent of what looked like scrambled egg was congealing in the center of the Formica table. A box of chocolates lay open and ransacked in the middle of the mess. A fork was balanced on the edge of a chair.

Remembering the surveillance camera, Pippa snapped her head back and looked up. The thing stared down at her with its cold glass eye, the red Record light blinking ominously. She couldn't bear for Herb to witness himself like this. Every day she would wake up extra early; if there was evidence, she planned to clean it up, erase the tape. He would never know. Pippa wiped up the mess as fast as she could, scraped off a smear of dried egg yolk with her fingernail, her vision blurred with tears.

She went into the den and shut the door, then shoved the tape into the mouth of the VCR. Her heart was pumping wildly in her chest. Seen from above, in black and white, like so many holdup videos Pippa had watched on television, her kitchen seemed sinister, like a crime scene. Pippa fast-forwarded the tape. Nothing. Nothing. Then a figure in white sped by, right through the frame. Pippa rewound the tape and hit Play. The room was empty again. A muffled, banging sound emerged from the TV. Then, a woman shuffled into the kitchen. It was Pippa/not Pippa. The stranger walked with an eerie, graceless gait, her posture slumped, her gaze downcast. This creature disappeared from the screen, came back into the edge of it, and started stirring eggs in a frying pan. She then dumped the eggs on the table, sat down in a hunched position, and scraped forkfuls of them off the Formica, shoveling them into her mouth with mechanical motions. Pippa watched herself with incredulity and revulsion. There was something inhuman about the scene.

She smashed the bedroom door open with her fist. Herb sat up, stunned with sleep. 'What –' She was next to him, burrowing her head in his chest, her cheeks wet with tears. 'It's me,' she said. 'Herb, it's me –'

'Slow down, pal. What are we talking about here?'

'The chocolate cake. And the eggs, and – I saw it on the video, oh, it's horrible.' He held her like that for a while, stroking her head.

'I must be walking in my sleep,' she said.

'I don't remember any eggs.'

'This morning there were eggs. All over the table. She – I – dumped them on the table and – Oh, my God, this makes me feel insane.'

'Didn't you do it when you were a kid?'

'That was just a couple of times I walked around.' At fourteen, she would pace the upstairs hall of the rectory, her pillow under her arm, till her insomniac mother led her back to bed.

'You sleepwalking is a hell of a lot better than me being senile,' Herb said, rolling onto his side and drawing Pippa in, raising his knees so she was resting in a little chair of him. She felt his warmth along her back, tucked her feet between his warm, furry calves.

'I guess so.'

'Sleepwalkers are a dime a dozen, honey. You can't even get off a murder rap with that defense anymore. So don't get any ideas.' She was already feeling reassured. Herb had a way of casting light on muddled thoughts, dissipating the shadows. This rational viewpoint was inherited from his father, a darkly funny man who despised religion, all exaggeration, and musicals. He was the embodiment of deadpan. Herb's mother had died of cancer when he was two; for years his father was a loving, if gruff, protector. He owned a profitable appliance store in Queens until he lost his business in the spending vacuum of the depression. With economic ruin came a darkening of Mr Lee's humor. Ribbing of his intelligent son turned to bullying and, finally, a bitter, brutal dismissiveness of Herb as an effete intellectual, a fag even. For much as he pitied the dupes that looked to God as a balm to their wounded spirits, Mr Lee reserved his special disdain for those who thought they were better than other people just because they read books. Herb was hurt by this rejection at first, but mercifully it absolved him of feeling guilty for bettering his old man. He left for college on a scholarship at nineteen, alone in the world, determined never to be bullied by another human being for the rest of his life, his taste in literature already formed by the very man he had come to hate so much. He mistrusted extravagant metaphor, favored the driest prose. As Herb saw it, he was always having to dehumidify Pippa's mind.

She felt a touch against her tailbone, and then it was gone – then back again, insistent, like a creature pressing its nose against her back. She turned, closed her eyes, and kissed him.

She was lying beside Herb, her eyes still a bit puffy from crying, when there was a knock on the door. She knelt on the bed and peered out the window, pushing the curtain aside. It was Dot. 'Doesn't that woman have a phone?' Herb asked. Pippa pulled on her robe and walked into the kitchen.

'Hi!' purred Dot, standing on the threshold. She looked different this morning. Beneath the crazy network of sun worshipper's lines etched into her deflated skin, Pippa could discern the sweep of a strong jaw. Her brown eyes were sparkling. Dot must have been a knockout.

'You look lovely,' said Pippa.

'Are you kidding? I'm on my way to the beauty parlor. Have you been crying?' asked Dot.

'It's just allergies,' said Pippa. 'Would you like to come in?'

Dot's eyes rose to the surveillance camera, then back to Pippa. 'I came to invite you over to meet Chris,' she said. 'Herb is welcome too, of course, only I don't want to disturb him.'

'Chris?'

'My son. He's moved in with us. It's perfectly legal.'

'Of course it is.'

'I mean, in the charter it says you can have relatives under fifty stay for up to six months. I'm just inviting a few neighbors, you know. I don't want anyone to think we're sneaking around.'

'I would love to meet him. When should I come over?'

'Around four would be good. We can all have a drink and be home in time to make dinner. I hope you don't think it's rude that I'm not inviting everyone over to eat.'

'Not at all.'

'It's just, I hate cooking in large quantities. It never comes out.'

As Pippa closed the door, she tried not to wonder about Dot. She sensed a tragic shadow there, a wound. Pippa suffered from an excess of empathy. Sometimes, she found the mystery of other people almost unbearable to contemplate: rooms within rooms inside each of them, an endless labyrinth of contradictory qualities, memories, desires, mirroring one another like an Escher drawing, baffling as a conundrum. Kinder to perceive people as they wished to be seen. After all, that's what Pippa wanted for herself: to be accepted as she seemed.

Motherhood and Cigarettes

A little after four o'clock, Pippa meandered over to Dot's house carrying a bottle of wine she had been keeping in reserve and wondering if she could possibly be pregnant in spite of the vestigial coil still lodged in her uterus like astronaut litter abandoned on the moon. Yet, no, rare as sex with Herb was these days, precautions were still necessary; eggs were meant to be fulminating inside her in this twilight of her fertility. The thought of a new baby now seemed absurd, even suffocating, much as she had loved being pregnant, addicted as she had been to the smell of her babies' necks, the soft crowns of their heads. That room was shut and locked; she couldn't pry it open.

Herb had opted to stay home from the party. Visiting a former dentist, his wife, and their half-baked son was not his idea of a good time. Pippa walked slowly, looking up at the gnarled branches of an oak tree, dark leaves shivering against the flat, blue sky. She felt hollowed out in a pleasant, staring way. The nightmare of the videotape seemed far off, yet it had left an aftertaste: wind flattening a patch of high grass by the side of the road with a hiss, an old man straining to pedal by her on a bicycle – everything that happened around her seemed to be gathering portent, like a fluffy white cloud augmenting itself, building up into a mountainous, darkening tower that threatened aircraft and frightened house pets with its ominous rumbling. She stopped and looked at the number of the house behind her. 1675. She had overshot the Nadeaus'. She backtracked and went up their front walk, identical to her own but for a large ceramic toadstool in the center of the front lawn. It was painted glossy red, with yellow spots on it. She knocked on the metal frame of the screen door. There was no answer, so she pushed the door open and walked into a layout just like her own but with a strikingly different décor.

The Nadeaus' living room was a visual explosion. Red ivy crawled up the wallpaper, the couch was paisley, the armchairs were various shades of pastel. A miniature Victorian town was laid out on a mahogany dresser: tiny, cast-metal buildings – dry goods store, church, train depot – lined a sinuous railroad track. A glossy red steam engine shuttled along the track in a joyless mechanical loop. Every other usable surface in the room was jammed with photographs. Faces upon faces crammed up against one another: generations of babies, schoolchildren, old people, soldiers, brides from every decade since 1910. Pippa tried to take it all in, her eyes darting around the room like an alarmed bird, seeking a place to rest. At last her gaze alighted on Dot herself, sitting stiffly in a peach silk armchair in the corner, her chartreuse blouse and white slacks ironed, her hair a single, shining blond wave. She was staring ahead with a fixed expression. Pippa came up to her.

'Hi, Dot,' she said.

Dot looked up at her with a steady, glittering stare. 'Everyone is out back,' she said hoarsely.

'Is everything all right?' Pippa asked.

'He won't come out,' Dot said.

'Your son?'

'He's staying in his room. Can you imagine? A man of thirty-five locks himself in his room when his parents throw him a party?' Someone laughed outside. Pippa glanced out the plate-glass window. A few people were on the patio, talking. Johnny, Dot's husband, was listening to an ancient man, a drink in his hand, his head cocked. Johnny was short, bullish, slightly bowlegged. He had rosy, healthy-looking skin.

Dot stood up unsteadily and took the wine bottle from Pippa. 'It's cold! You shouldn't have. Let's open it.' Pippa followed Dot into the kitchen. Dot pulled out the cork and poured them each a glass of wine. 'To motherhood,' Dot said, knocking back half the glass.

Outside, Pippa met a few of her neighbors. There were a couple of retired dentists, a saxophonist, a former chiropractor, a tiny woman who had written a book on child psychology. The sax player, a widower, was clearly hitting on the voluptuous wife of the chiropractor. They were both in their eighties. Pippa took it all in, stored it so she could tell Herb later. Pippa was a little high from the wine. She leaned back against the Nadeaus' trellis and felt her hips loosen up, her left leg swing open. Living in Marigold Village made her feel youthful. She was once again the youngest woman around, just as she had been when she and Herb had first been together. Watching a bent old woman laugh a few feet away, she flexed the strong muscles in her calves, stood up straighter, pressing her breasts against her thin blouse. She felt the familiar arrogance of youth, as if her age made her superior, as if it were to her credit.

Johnny Nadeau ambled over to her with his stiff-legged walk. 'Hello, Pippa, glad you could come. A little eye candy,' he said, winking.

'Thanks for having me, Johnny.'

He leaned in to her and whispered emphatically: 'I'd appreciate if you could keep an eye on Dot.' She could smell pretzels on his breath. 'She's having a hard time. I know she talks to you.'

'Sure,' said Pippa, glancing at the spot where Dot had been. 'Where is she?'

'She went back inside. I told her this was a bad idea,' he said, shaking his head. Pippa started walking toward the sliding door. Again, the stage whisper: 'Get her to drink a Coca-Cola.'

Pippa walked into the living room. It was empty. She peeked into the kitchen. No Dot. She heard arguing, crying, coming from somewhere down the hall. She followed the sound, walking gingerly. Pippa imagined Dot and the half-baked son locked in a murderous embrace, Dot trying to drag him out to the party, the doughy son resisting, squeezing the breath out of her till she hung, limp and immobile, off his pasty arm. Pippa came to a bedroom door. They were in there. She could hear them. She knocked tentatively. The voices went silent.

'Dot?' she said.

'Who is it?' It was a man's voice.

'It's Pippa Lee. I . . . was just looking for Dot.'

There was a fumbling noise, then the door swung open. A powerfully built man in his thirties, with a thin, ashen face and broken nose, stared through Pippa with a look of blank aggression, his mind on something else. His meaty, naked torso was tattooed with an intricately painted Christ. The Lord was portrayed in color, from the waist up; he was bare-chested and had very large wings. Pippa peered behind the son and saw Dot sitting on the bed. Her eyes were red from crying.

'Dot,' Pippa said, struggling to keep her voice even. 'Johnny asked me to find you.'

'Look at me,' said Dot. 'I can't go out there.' She blew her nose into a large tissue.

Pippa gamely held out her hand to the son. 'I'm Pippa Lee,' she said.

'Chris,' said the son, taking her hand with a surprisingly gentle grip. 'Pleased to meet you. I'm sorry you had to be party to our little . . . thing, here . . .' He now began rummaging through a duffel bag and pulled out a wrinkled shirt. Pippa noticed that the Christ's wings extended over the man's shoulders and partway down his back. Dot watched her decorated son with a sly expression as he tugged on the shirt, buttoned the buttons. 'Take care of my mother,' he said, fixing Pippa with an alarmingly frank gaze and backing up toward the wall. 'I have to go.' And with this, Chris climbed out the window and strode away. He had a rocking gait and leaned far back as he walked, chin tucked in, arms slightly curled, as though ready to be attacked. He opened the door of the yellow truck, swung himself onto the driver's seat, and sped off.

'He was such a sweet little boy,' said Dot helplessly, shaking her head. 'You can't imagine.'

*

Several days passed, and, though Chris Nadeau's bright yellow truck sped by Pippa on the road a few times, she heard nothing from Dot. She thought that perhaps shame about the scene at the party had made their friendship impossible. The son was scary. Poor Dot. To her surprise, Pippa found herself missing Dot a little bit. She wondered if she should call and see if she was okay, or if that would be awkward. The sleepwalking seemed to have evaporated. No new messes had appeared in the kitchen. Pippa felt a calm wash over her. The days passed in the quietest possible way. Ben called from the city every Sunday. Grace was in Paris, recovering from two weeks photographing in Kabul.

Pippa was still baffled as to how it had happened. One minute, it seemed, Grace was photographing dog shows for the *Hartford Courant*. The next, she was capturing horrendous images of maimed children, screaming women that showed up in *The New York Times*. Pippa was amazed by Grace's fierce pursuit of the truth at all costs. Yet a part of her wondered, as she stared into the eyes of yet another terrified person running through a sea of dust, if there wasn't something a little bit ruthless about photographing people in such distress. She hadn't asked the question of her daughter, but there it was anyway: Was there a moment when you had to choose between photographing a person and helping them? But at least she was doing something, Pippa thought. Drawing attention to. Herself. No. Not fair. To conflicts, injustices. As opposed to Pippa. Oh well, she thought as she thumbed through a luxuriously illustrated cookbook: osso buco. Lamb Milanese. Spaghetti alle vongole. At least Herb was appreciative. He loved being taken care of.

He had found a book written by an unknown, a high school history teacher in Idaho. It had come to him in a plain manila envelope, the address typed on a manual typewriter. When he saw it, he said, This is either a lunatic or the real thing. As it turned out, the book inside was that rare beast every publishing house is always praying for: an Easy Read of Quality. It was a historical romance, told in excruciating detail. Deeply moving. Expressive language. Would make a sweeping, epic film. Herb was serious about literature. He published most of the few giants left. But he was also a businessman, and receiving a novel like this in the mail was like winning the lottery. He could publish ten poets with the money this behemoth would bring in. It needed work, sure, but Herb was confident that, with some cutting and reshaping, it could be damn strong. He read the last of twelve hundred pages, folded his hands on the manuscript, and closed his eyes. He felt Pippa leaning over him as she bent to pick up his empty glass.

'I found a book,' he said.

'Oh, great,' said Pippa.

'A real cash cow,' he said.

'Since when do you say "cash cow"?'

'I never found one before, so I never said it.'

'What's it about?'

'War. Romance. Bad weather.'

'Is it good?'

'It's a certain kind of good. It's lowbrow for highbrows. Or highbrow for lowbrows. It's perfect summer reading for people who own multimillion-dollar beach homes.'

'That used to be us.'

'Not us,' he said.

Pippa brought the glass into the kitchen. It was so strange, she thought. The closer Herb got to death, the more he thought about money.

Grace

Grace's jolt into the rarefied world of reportage photographers was unforeseen by everyone in the family, especially Grace. In college, she majored in Spanish with a minor in photography. The summer after she graduated, Ben took off to backpack through Europe with his girlfriend, Stephanie, also a future lawyer. Though the twins had gone to different colleges, Grace had assumed that, when they both graduated, she and Ben would live together – at least for a summer, to recapture the gleeful conspiracy of their life at home. But Ben felt he ought to grow up, become a man, be sane, not frolic around with his sister. So off he went to Europe with Stephanie, that loyal hound. Grace knew that Ben loved Stephie for what she wasn't (neurotic, blunt, alluring, hilarious) as much as for what she was (constant, sweet, accommodating yet intelligent – a sort of modern-day Olivia de Havilland in *Gone with the Wind*). In essence, she knew her brother had chosen a girl as unlike herself as possible.

So, after graduation, uninterested in rooming with any of her college friends who were swarming into Brooklyn, Grace rented herself a one-bedroom apartment in Spanish Harlem with high, arched windows and mucus yellow linoleum on the floors, hoping to improve her Spanish and think about what to do next. She had enough money from her parents to avoid a job, for the summer anyway, if she lived frugally. She spent the first two weeks wandering around the neighborhood, picking through tag sale items laid out on the street: used communion dresses, worn paperbacks, the occasional comb – and eating rice and beans with fried plantains at the counter of her local restaurant while reading biographies of Lee Miller and Lawrence of Arabia. She furnished her apartment with two beanbag chairs (one maraschino red, one Fanta orange) and an ornate white wrought-iron bedstead. She didn't talk much to anyone. She enjoyed this removal from her surroundings even as she was immersed in them. She felt mute and contented, loaded with potential, yet entirely unproductive.

She came to know every nook and cranny of her block; the dusty windows of the Assembly of God meetinghouse on the second floor of number 1125, the musty used bookstore in the basement of 1130, the botanica on the corner, which advertised cures for lovesickness, homesickness, and 'most ailments of the soul and body.' The bodega on the corner of 120th Street was run by a puffy-eyed, garrulous Dominican man and his taciturn grandson, a melancholic who moped behind the counter, his haunted, dark eyes, wasted face, and pointed goatee making him look like a figure out of an El Greco painting. The same five old men sat on folding chairs outside the bodega every day watching pedestrians, making bets on everything from the racetrack to who was going to step on a particularly large crack in the sidewalk as they passed by. Young women and girls walked proudly down the street in tight clothes, glossy hair scraped back from their exhausted faces, pushing strollers with babies or toddlers lolling inside. The wizened, high-haired lady who ran the Laundromat stood outside smoking and chatting with her neighbors when she wasn't folding sheets inside the picture window.

Grace came to think of that stretch of pavement on Lexington between East 120th and East 122nd streets as a world of its own. Though some people on the block had come to recognize Grace and said hello when they passed her or when she walked into their shops, she still felt relatively invisible. She was not a part of the life of the block; she was an accepted observer. Looking at her, you couldn't say she blended in, particularly. She had wild, blond hair that fell in angry ringlets around a pointed, intelligent face. Her body was tall, thin, and athletic, her breasts small and compact. Men always noticed her but rarely approached her; there was something mannish in her movements. From behind, with her slim hips and muscular shoulders, her relaxed posture, she could have been mistaken for a long-haired boy.

One night late, a bottle shattered in the street and woke Grace up. A man called out in Spanish; another man answered. Their arguing voices echoed in the cavernous apartment. Grace walked barefoot across the linoleum, trying to make out what was being said. A young woman was pleading; she had tears in her voice. Grace stood inches away from the windowsill, so she could not be seen, and peered down into the street. The three protagonists of the fight were leaning against two cars parked a few yards away from each other. She recognized the El Greco grandson of the bodega owner. She had never seen him so animated. He was flailing his arms, gesturing, calling the other man, an older, stocky fellow with his feet planted very far apart, 'a liar and a fool' in Spanish. A slight girl of around fifteen, whom Grace had seen pushing her baby up and down the block, was hanging on to the grandson's arm, trying to pull him away. Several onlookers had gathered in a semicircle to watch the proceedings.

Grace stood transfixed by this dangerous and real drama unfolding below, as though in a box at the theater. For a long time, the two men were in a stalemate, the El Greco grandson shrieking hysterically at the thickset stranger, the girl alternately trying to calm him down and yelling at him to shut up, the stranger walking up to the pair menacingly, then returning to the hood of his car, only to be pelted with a new round of insults from the El Greco grandson. In spite of this posturing, the stranger didn't seem very committed to the argument; he even looked around him a few times, as if for a more comfortable seat. But finally, the grandson said something that got his goat. Grace didn't catch the meaning, but whatever it was, it was the last straw. The stranger charged the grandson, flinging the girl aside like a doll, and laid the boy flat with one punch. Then he walked away, shaking his head. A few people gathered around the grandson, who sat up slowly and, shaking off their solicitude, limped away in the opposite direction.

The next morning Grace woke up thinking about the Minolta her parents had given her for graduation. She took the camera out of its case and loaded it with film. That was the morning she began to photograph in earnest. She spent the next two months documenting every waking hour of her block. The people already knew her, so they tolerated her lens poking at them, even invited her into their apartments occasionally. She photographed everything, everyone she could – the Assembly of God Sunday service, the affable bodega owner, the El Greco grandson, the old men sitting outside the bodega, the Laundromat lady. She built her portfolio up image by image, photographing day and night as if pursued. The resulting stack of pictures showed obsessive commitment and a sharp eye. She got an appointment with the editor of the *Hartford Courant*, a paper she had heard was open to hiring young photographers. They took her on. She spent the fall and winter chasing fire trucks and photographing orange tape stretched around suburban houses where murders had occurred; by the following summer, she was on a plane bound for Louisiana to cover Hurricane Katrina for the *Courant* with a senior colleague. She slept just a few hours a night for the entire two weeks; there wasn't a moment of that tragedy she wanted to miss. The trip was oddly blessed for her; images of horror and hopelessness spiked with humor seemed to cohere inside her lens again and again. She couldn't seem to help being at the right place at the right time. The pictures she brought back were surreal: three children wearing rubber Halloween masks of George Washington, Elvis Presley, and Chucky discover the corpse of an aged man in an alley; a shivering dog stands perched on an island of garbage, surrounded by floating dolls; a big woman dances around in the remains of her decimated living room, wallpaper hanging from the walls like shreds of skin. Grace returned to the *Courant* a star. Within two years she was on the staff of Getty Images, touching down in Kabul.

Grace was perplexed by what seemed to others to be talent yet felt to her like something else. Her luck was uncanny to her. It was as though she herself was creating the images, dreaming them onto the emulsion. It was, perhaps, the way she was able to forget herself, to disappear, to become transparent when she photographed, that made it so hard for her to take credit for her own work. Sometimes, she was swallowed up by the experience so completely that she could not remember having taken the pictures at all. Yet she had, of course, and anything paranormal about her new chosen profession was, she knew, adolescent hokum she would never have shared with a soul, except her twin, whom she treated with the brutal frankness, the mocking acuity she reserved for her own internal life.

Ben was, for Grace, an extension of her self. Some of what she was doing by working so hard, she knew, or rather saw dimly in some back room of her mind like a mouse one perceives scurrying along a wall out of the corner of one's eye, was getting away from Ben by surpassing him. Their relationship was absolutely perfect. It was so perfect, in fact, that Grace needed no one else. She had not, as the psychotherapist she saw for a few months in college, Dr Sarah Kreutzfeldt, put it, 'individuated completely.' Grace's chief complaint, when she first availed herself of the University Health Services, was that she couldn't fall in love. She thought there must be something wrong with her. There had been one obvious opportunity: an intelligent, interesting, funny boy with sparkling eyes and a caved-in, question mark-shaped torso. She kept teetering on the brink of love with him, and even spent blissful hours in the zone of extreme fondness. But all it took was one flabby joke, a botched allusion, a moment of strained sincerity, and she felt a leaden seal forming in her gut, cutting her off from the suddenly former object of her affection as swiftly as a pair of scissors severing two sausage links. Back to square one.

She blamed Ben for it all – smart, funny, endearing, infuriating Ben. No one would ever make her laugh so much; no one could

peer at the world with the same good-natured, even loving deri-
sion. After a couple of weeks of looking at this same observation
from different angles, her sessions with Dr Kreutzfeldt were drying
up. Grace was embarrassed by the triviality of her problem. She
chided herself for even initiating the therapy, but now she felt
obliged to keep it up. She began to resent Dr Kreutzfeldt. She
became sullen and uncommunicative during the sessions, staring
out the window at the students walking from the library to the
dorms, the dorms to the math building.

This behavior piqued Sarah Kreutzfeldt's interest. She had
always sensed some subterranean explosion in the girl, a mine
going off so far inside her that even she was unaware of it.
When Grace first stomped into her office, she was surprised.
This girl did not seem like Larken material. A very small university, Larken catered to the privileged painters, writers, critics,
poets, and performance artists of the future. The teaching was
not so much rigorous as expansive, the teachers stretching their
courses to the point of deformity in order to encompass the
whimsy of the students. Terms like *participatory* and *student-
centered* took top billing in the school brochure. Most of the
students had a vague, haunted look, like possums disturbed from
their burrows in the middle of the day. They walked through
campus slowly, in a haze of half-digested ideas, each convinced
of his or her own inherent flair. By contrast, Grace had a sharp,
intense countenance. Her eyes were very focused; her walk was
a march. She seemed hyperawake.

Dr Kreutzfeldt knew there was something besides her twin at
work in this girl's psyche. She wasn't sick; she was stuck. There
was some knot in her that needed to be loosened. Not sure where
to begin, Dr Kreutzfeldt started with the obvious: the parents.
Grace shrugged and spoke of Herb with affection, Pippa with a
mix of regret and disdain. This mother was clearly a doormat,
Dr Kreutzfeldt thought, internally shaking her head. She never
would understand some women. The kids grow up, and then what?

Yet she sensed strong emotion in Grace when she talked about her mother. Her cheeks flushed, she looked away. Kreutzfeldt sensed an emotional morass obscured by irony cool as a blanket of metal filings. Something had happened with the mother.

Over the weeks, gently, shifting her weight slightly in her armchair, her attractive, full face tilted slightly as she spoke, Dr Kreutzfeldt guided Grace back, again and again, to what she saw as a kind of crossroads of character. For the first few years of her life, Grace had been extremely close to her mother. She remembered screaming when Pippa went out to dinner, craving her smell, her embrace, treasuring the time they spent together playing on the beach or just staring out the window. Yet by the time Grace was eight or nine, a vast, arid divide had opened up between them. Dr Kreutzfeldt kept returning to the period she had come to refer to as 'the turning point' in Grace's relationship with her mother, hoping that some illuminating memory would spring from the girl's mind. But there was nothing. And then one day, out of nowhere it seemed, after a long silence, Grace looked out the window and said softly, 'I don't think my mother likes me very much.'

Dr Kreutzfeldt was taken aback. 'But she seems to be almost slavishly devoted to you,' she said.

'She is,' said Grace. 'But there's a part of her that she always held back. Not with Ben. Just with me.'

'And you are angry with her for rejecting you,' offered Dr Kreutzfeldt.

'I suppose,' said Grace with a slight sneer. And then, turning, half-laughing, she said in her mocking tone, 'Am I cured now?'

Pippa stared out the window of Herb's Mercedes and thought about Grace. It had been three months since she'd been to see them, before her trip to Afghanistan, her second in a year. Pippa had butterflies in her stomach. She always did, these days, when she was going to see her daughter. Seeing Ben was like putting on your favorite old pair of jeans. Seeing Grace was like . . . like bumping into someone you had a crush on. No, Pippa thought, that can't be it. And yet it was, a little.

Herb had chosen the Gotham Bar and Grill so he could have a decent meal. The kids had loved to go there around Christmas when they were little. It was absurdly expensive, but there was something reassuring about the heavy cloth on the tables, the superfluous busboys, the quiet conversations, the fine silk and wool of the customers' suits. It felt like going back in time. Herb and Pippa were early, as they always were, and Pippa was teasingly trying to distance the bread basket from Herb's big hands. She saw Grace through the window as she approached. She had cut her wild blond hair short. It looked like underbrush. Her nose looked sharper somehow, a little beakish, Pippa thought, as Grace shoved the heavy door open with too much force, walked up the steps, and stood raking the room with her cool gaze. Pippa waved at her, and Grace approached with long strides, unwinding a scarlet silk scarf from around her neck. Herb stood up and hugged Grace hard. Grace then leaned across the table and brushed Pippa's cheek with her lips.

'Am I late?' she asked.

'I had time to eat all the bread,' said Herb.

'Your hair looks wonderful,' said Pippa.

'Thanks,' Grace said, running her hand through the light blond mop.

'So. Tell us,' said Herb.

'Oh, Dad, give me a second. Ben said to start without him. He's stuck in the library. He'll be here as soon as he can.'

'It must be that paper,' said Herb.

'Yes. *That paper*,' said Grace, making loving fun of her brother. 'Can I have lamb chops, please? I'm starving.' They ordered for themselves and for Ben, then Grace put her portfolio on the table.

'These are just work prints, but anyway it gives you an

idea . . .' She set the pile of photographs in front of Herb. Pippa had to look at them upside down. As Herb finished examining each picture, he slid it over to her. In one, a little boy bent over another, prone child, as if protecting her, his face pinched with fright. In another, a man pushed a bicycle, his large, dark, haunted eyes staring into the camera. The front wall of the house behind him had been entirely torn off; on the second floor, a bed, chair, and mirror were arranged like a stage set, open to the world.

'Were you alone when you took these?' Pippa asked. She could feel Grace bristle.

'No, I hitched a ride with Giles Oppenheim.' Two-time winner of the Pulitzer Prize, Oppenheim was a legend among war photographers.

'How did you manage that?' asked Herb.

'It's pretty common, people look out for each other there.'

'Well, you've got courage, we know that much,' said Herb. He was nearly exploding with pride, and Grace knew it.

'These are the best yet,' said Pippa.

'Thanks,' said Grace, little red spots appearing on her pale cheeks.

Ben arrived, pleased to have his lunch laid out for him. 'Has she told you about the bomb?' he asked, pleasantly.

'Ben,' said Grace.

'What bomb?' asked Pippa.

'She was with that Oppenheim fellow, and the translator, and they heard a bomb go off down the street, and Oppenheim tried to drag her left, but she ran down an alley to the right, and he and the translator followed her, and a van exploded right where he was trying to take her; if they had gone left they would have been pulverized. So now she thinks it's destiny.'

Ben was lighthearted in his delivery, but he was furious with his sister, who was becoming, he felt, dangerously, arrogantly brave. Herb and Pippa just sat there, taking in the story. Pippa felt sweat coming up on her brow, a wave of nausea.

Grace looked at Ben, her face set. 'Can't you ever just *not say* something?'

'Well, it seemed kind of important,' said Ben.

'Just use your common sense,' said Herb quietly. 'That's all I ask.' Then, turning to Ben: 'So when are you going to let me read this famous paper?' Ben began to talk about his course work. Grace listened to their conversation in a distanced way, her chin resting on her fist, and Pippa observed her daughter. In spite of the camaraderie Grace seemed to have with her colleagues in the field, Pippa sensed a growing remoteness in her that she found alarming. It seemed to be harder and harder for Grace to return from her photographic odysseys. She was entering other, mirror worlds so violent and intense that the West must seem cold, trivial, and meaningless in comparison. Grace was sealed inside her own experiences, unable to relay what she had seen and felt; the photographs bore mute witness to stories Pippa would have loved to hear every detail of, but she didn't dare ask for fear of the silent rebuff she knew she'd get from her daughter in return for meddling. And to think – such a short time ago, Grace had been a little girl! Within this severe young woman, Pippa could discern, flashing in and out like an image in a hologram, Grace's former, child selves. It was so lonely, knowing things about her children that they no longer remembered. Layers of experience eroded from their minds but petrified in her own. As often happened when she saw Grace, Pippa remembered a day which, she had come to believe, had changed her daughter's life.

The twins were eight. She had decided to take them to the Dairy Queen on Sixth Avenue, after their piano lessons. It was the first spring day after a frigid winter, and the warm air felt liquid against Pippa's skin. People on the street moved languorously, as if drugged with relief. Pippa looked down at the twins, their messy, light blond hair shining in the sun, and swelled with gratitude for her good fortune. When they drifted into the ice cream store, a lady of about sixty in a blue skirt and loafers, white socks pulled up past her ankles, gray hair held back in a ponytail, stood at the counter beside a dark-haired girl of about the twins' age. The lady was saying, in broken English, 'How much is a milk-shake?' The bored man behind the counter told her. The little girl beside the woman had a tight, embarrassed smile on her face as the older woman counted out her change. When the lady saw that Pippa and the twins were waiting, she moved aside to let them order, scraping her coins a few inches to the left with her cupped palm. Pippa asked for two vanilla cones and gave the man a twenty. As he made change, Pippa noticed Grace gaping at the lady as she sifted through her little pile of coins, squinting up at the board with the prices on it anxiously, the little girl by her side stiff with shame. Pippa poked Grace, but she wouldn't look away.

'And how much is a soda?' asked the lady, smiling. Her dark eyes were shining with kindness and a hint of apology for the fuss she was making. The man gave her a price, and she went back to counting her change. Pippa could feel tears coming to her eyes. This poor woman had taken her granddaughter out for a treat, and now she couldn't afford it. The clerk gave Pippa her change, and she crammed the bills into her wallet furtively, wondering if it would humiliate the lady if she offered to pay for the little girl's dessert. She decided against it; it would be condescending.

The man handed Pippa the cones. The soft white cream looked perfect, plastic, shiny, like ice cream in a commercial. Pippa gave Ben his, Grace hers. Ben licked his hungrily, but Grace didn't touch hers. Pippa began to move toward the door. Ben followed. Grace stood stock-still, glaring at the ground, clutching her cone. 'Grace,' Pippa said softly. Abruptly, Grace bolted toward the little dark-haired girl, stood a foot away from her, and offered her the ice cream. The girl stared at the gift, uncomprehending. Grace stood still, the ice cream cone in her fist raised like a sword in the hand of a statue. The lady said something to the little girl in some foreign tongue, and the child took the cone shyly, casting her eyes to the floor. Then Grace turned and fled the Dairy Queen. Pippa rushed out behind her. She could hear the woman calling out a thank-you as the glass door sighed shut behind her. When Pippa finally caught up with Grace, halfway down the block, the child's face was flushed, her gray eyes clouded with fury.

'That was a lovely thing to do,' Pippa said.

'No it wasn't,' Grace said. She didn't want to talk about it after that. She was quiet on the cab ride home and all through dinner. Pippa knew that something had changed in her child that day. She'd become angry at her own good fortune.

*

Sponge, spray cleaner, water, mop: time to clean the kitchen! Pippa liked things neat, but she was naturally chaotic. She had to use all her concentration to bend her mind to the task of cleaning, like a high wind forcing a tall tree to the ground. One stray thought and she would wander away from her scrubbing, end up staring at hummingbirds through her binoculars or checking a recipe for spaghetti alla primavera, only to return to the kitchen forty minutes later, surprised to see the dishes still piled high. This morning, however, Pippa was keeping an image of a perfectly neat kitchen in mind, trying to replicate it in reality. She took everything off the counter, sponged it down, then replaced the vitamin bottles and condiments, carefully lining them up. She wiped down the stove, scrubbed the pan encrusted with Herb's chicken sausage, emptied the dishwasher, putting away clean dishes and flatware, then filled it again with dirty dishes and flatware. She poured blue and white speckled dishwashing powder into the little rectangular box, slid its door shut till it clicked, turned on the machine, selecting 'heavy duty wash' because there was a pan in there. She swept the floor, mopped it. She wiped out the sink, even opened up the fridge and threw out everything that looked sad or rotten. She made a list: eggs, soy milk, yogurt, aluminum foil. Grape-Nuts.

She folded the list, tucked it into the zip-up compartment inside her purse, and walked out onto the patio. Herb was on the phone. He looked at her expectantly.

'I'm going shopping. Is there anything you need?' she asked.

He shook his head, waved, and went back to his phone call. He was talking about the book. Pippa wondered who the author of the cash cow might be. She walked through the livingroom, out the door, got into the car, and froze.

The floor of the car was littered with cigarette butts. There must have been ten of them, stamped right into the carpeting. Pippa had quit smoking twenty years ago. The smell of smoke made her throat close up. Herb had never smoked cigarettes, and he had given up cigars on the advice of his heart specialist. So what the hell was this? She picked up the butts, dropped them into a Baggie she kept in the glove compartment, and hurried back into the house to tell Herb. He was still on the phone. She lingered in the living room for a few seconds, waiting. The car had been open. It could have been teenagers, some kids from the nearby town, out having fun. It could have been Chris Nadeau, in an oblique act of revenge for coming upon him as she had. Or it could have been Pippa. She felt her cheeks growing hot. And if it was she, if she had walked in her sleep, and smoked in the car, she might have driven the car. She found this thought terrifying.

Where did she get the cigarettes? A feeling of bottomless panic came over her; it felt like she was standing in an elevator with the cord cut, going down – down – down. Herb, unaware, continued: 'Well, Phil, you can do two things,' he was saying. 'You can get an agent, I can recommend an agent to you. You'll need one eventually anyway, you're a writer now. Or you can hold off, make this deal on your own, forget about their cut. The good news is, you get the entire advance. The other side of the coin is, an agent will be more interested in you if he has this book, and he'll be loyal, because you're gonna make him a lot of money.'

Pippa, feeling slightly dizzy, turned and walked out of the house, got into the car, then drove a very slow mile to the convenience store. They stocked simple groceries, and it was the only place in Marigold Village that sold *The New York Times*. She walked in, still wearing her sunglasses. Forgetting about her list, she distractedly picked up the newspaper, eggs, a packet of pancake mix. Her hands were shaking. She walked to the register and looked up. There was Chris Nadeau, his hair wet and slicked back, face freshly shaved, thick brows like dark brush marks on light skin, lips chapped. He smelled of aftershave. There was something hulking about him, strength coiled so tight it looked like relaxation. 'Pippa Lee, right?'

'Oh, hi,' she said, taking off her glasses. 'You got a job already.'

'I'm working my way to the top,' said Chris.

'It's a beautiful day,' said Pippa.

'I'm trying not to notice,' he said, punching in the items on the cash register; his fingernails were bitten down to the quick, Pippa noticed. Her eyes then wandered to the wall of cigarettes displayed behind him; she felt a sudden impulse to smoke clutching at her chest.

'Oh, and, ah – a packet of . . . Marlboro Lights. Please.'

Chris turned around and found the cigarettes. 'Costly habit,' he said.

'It's just – I don't really smoke,' she said. And then, a thought dawning, 'You don't work here at night, do you?'

'I haven't yet,' he said. 'Why do you ask?'

She felt relieved.

'It's open all night, and I always thought it would be a terrible job, just waiting . . . all night, for someone to buy . . . you know, cigarettes, or something.' Tears were starting to come to her eyes, the breath catching in her throat. Chris looked at her with a patient, listening gaze, his face expressionless. She felt completely exposed before him. His total lack of mannerisms was almost offensive in its directness. Mercifully, her emotion began to recede.

'Matches?' he asked.

'Please. How's your mother?'

'Recovering,' he said. 'I'm sorry I skipped out on you the other day. I'm not a big party person.'

'I shouldn't have – I shouldn't have interrupted,' she said. A man in line behind her cleared his throat. She put some bills down, fumbled through her purse for exact change. 'Well,' she said. 'Tell Dot to call me, if she wants to.'

'You'll have to call her,' said Chris. 'She's too mortified.'

Pippa left the convenience store, got into the car, ripped open the cigarettes, pulled one out and lit up. As the smoke filled her lungs, she felt a tingling in her hands and lips. Everything she looked at – the steering wheel, her hand, the gas pump outside – seemed saturated with color and detail. She hung her arm out the window. Why am I doing this? she thought. Her eyes wandered to Chris, tallying up someone's purchases. What a strange young man. Seems bright, but . . . She was beginning to know what Dot meant. There was something not quite right about him. Chris looked up and saw her through the glass. She waved at him cheerfully, put out the cigarette, and drove away.

Sam Shapiro and Moira Dulles were coming over for dinner again. It was too hot for warm dishes, so Pippa poached a salmon, made potato salad with vinaigrette dressing, and served it all on the patio. After dinner, the four of them sat quietly eating strawberries, looking out at the small artificial lake in the golden light and listening to the crickets. 'Delicious strawberries, Pippa,' said Sam.

'I got them at the farm stand,' Pippa said, looking at him and thinking how he had changed over the years. The skin on his long neck had loosened and trembled now like a turkey's wattle. The point of his hawk's nose had been dulled, rounded somehow, as if worn away by the grindstone he'd kept it to for the past thirty years, writing twelve hours a day almost without fail, hounded by the stories in his head like Orestes by the Furies. His eyes, once liquid black like molten tar, now looked dead as coals. It was as though, by writing all his life, he had consumed himself, chunk by chunk, and now he was a host, a husk. Time and again, Sam took his life and the people in it, boiled it all down – skin, bones, all of it – till it was a paste the color, Pippa imagined, of whale blubber. Then he built up an image with this paste, a kind of complex frieze, a story made of human beings, human feelings, human memory.

The main problem Pippa had with Sam (much as she loved him as a friend) was that she suspected he needed his relationships to fail so he could use them later. He would be a monster, she thought, if he wasn't more merciless with himself than with anyone else. But it was he who jumped into the caldron first, every time. To be cooked down and rise again; that was Sam's endless, exhausting destiny. A writer, and no more. The hopefulness had gone out of him, she thought sadly. But that was the deal he had made: in exchange for a real life, he had been given nine novels, two of them classics, the rest excellent, his immortality almost assured. Still, she pitied her old friend. And she felt sorry for Moira for having fallen in love with him; he would never give her what she wanted. She was too needy. The trick with Sam, Pippa knew, would be to make his life so appealing, such a pleasure, that he could not but turn toward it, and away from himself – at least a little bit. But then, she thought, Moira is a writer, too. So maybe they understand each other. She sighed and noticed Chris Nadeau's yellow truck parked across the way. She wondered what was going on inside the Nadeau house at that moment.

'How's the novel coming?' asked Herb.

'I'm only a hundred pages in,' said Sam. 'I don't even know if it'll work yet.'

'Excuse me for a minute,' Pippa said. She went to the bathroom, locked herself in, opened the window, and took the cigarettes out from behind Herb's blood pressure medication. She blew the smoke through the screen, watched it expand and disappear into the dark air. Then she brushed her teeth.

She came back to the patio with a slab of pistachio halvah, feeling toxic from the cigarette and berating herself for smoking. Moira sighed deeply and craned her neck to see the sky, drawing her knees up to her heavy bust and clutching them to her, her large, black, kohl-rimmed eyes glazing over with wonder. All of Moira's gestures and reactions had an element of self-consciousness. At twenty-four, she had won the coveted Yale Younger Poets prize. From there she'd gone on to publish a few volumes of surprisingly vitriolic poetry, her private life a brushfire of failed romances. In her middle thirties now, she clung to the demeanor of near-constant astonishment that had clashed so beautifully with her intellect in her early years. Not that Moira was old. No, she was a good deal younger than Pippa. Among the aging literary set she circulated in, she was a bombshell. Pippa found her endearing – and occasionally pitiful. She was irresponsible and neurotic, a grown woman without children, without health insurance even, still searching for love with the reckless hopefulness of a twenty-year-old. Yet occasionally, Pippa found herself envying Moira's chaotic, self-centered life.

'Is that a bat?' Moira asked, squinting.

'Yes,' said Herb.

'"Like a glove, a black glove thrown up at the light,"' said Moira. 'Who said that? What's his name.'

'The sex fiend,' said Sam. 'Mr Lawrence.'

'You should talk,' said Herb.

'And he got it wrong, too. Look at that. Does that look like a black glove to you?' asked Sam. They all looked up. 'It's a fucking *bat*.'

'Ben used to subscribe to a magazine about bats, remember?' Pippa said to Herb.

'Oh, yeah,' he said, squinting in recollection.

'Look how frenetic the fluttering wings are; that's how you can tell it's not a bird,' said Moira.

'No,' said Sam. 'It's the way it changes direction so fast – like a stunt kite.'

49

'That's good.' Herb chuckled. 'A stunt kite.' Sam tucked his chin into his neck, content; Herb never said anything was good unless he meant it.

'Do they really get in your hair?' asked Moira.

Sam tossed his head. 'Could you maybe just once come up with an idea that isn't a cliché?' Moira looked at him, an incredulous expression on her face. 'Just kidding,' he said. 'You're an original, baby, and don't you forget it.'

'Fuck you, too,' said Moira.

Pippa stood up. 'Decaf, anyone?' she asked in mock-stewardess style.

Moira stood up as well, and followed Pippa into the kitchen. By the time they got to the stove, she was sobbing. 'Every time I open my mouth, he puts me down. I can't take it any more. He's such a *prick*.'

Pippa sighed. Sam was cruel to his women. Everyone knew that. She'd seen him gnaw through a handful of them over the years.

'That's just the way he is sometimes. He has a mean streak. Maybe if you just laughed along?'

'I've been laughing for four years. Now I'm crying.'

'Are you talking about breaking up?'

'We're not talking about anything. Sam is so involved with his novel, he barely looks up. I'm having all of our discussions with myself.'

'Have you found ... someone else?' Pippa knew Moira well enough to guess she wouldn't think of leaving a man as powerful and desirable as Sam Shapiro unless she had a replacement in the wings. Gifted as she was, this poet needed big men.

Moira looked down at her hands. 'No ... I mean –' Then, pressing her palms against her eyes, 'Oh, Pippa, I'm so confused!'

That night in bed, as Herb tried to read and Pippa rubbed cream between the backs of her hands, she mused, 'I bet you Moira's having an affair.'

'What makes you say that?' Herb asked.

'She's talking about leaving Sam, but she's terrified of being on her own. It just adds up.'

'Maybe she wants you to think she's having an affair so you'll tell me, and I'll tell Sam, and he'll pay more attention to her.'

'Do you really think Moira is that conniving?'

'That's what women are like.'

'Devious?'

'It's instinct. Survival of the fittest. Of all people, you should know.'

'Never mind.'

'Does that mean I get to go to sleep now?' Herb said, yawning and putting his reading glasses in their case. 'Since reading is clearly out.'

'I still think she's having an affair,' said Pippa, turning out her light.

A Little Death

The office of Maxwell, Lee and Brewer Publishing was in New York, five surprisingly shabby, glassed-in rooms choked with books. In Herb's absence, the company was being run by Marianne Stapleton, a muscular, somewhat manic person with excellent taste and a penchant for self-doubt. She called Herb at least five times a day with questions.

'If I have an office,' Herb told Pippa, 'I give that maniac three hours a day when she can call me. The rest of the time, I'm retired.'

Though Marigold Village was a retirement community, there was office space available. Mostly rented out to businesses that catered to the residents, the smaller units were modestly priced. Pippa found Herb a room with an adjoining toilet that looked out onto the mini-mall. She got him a sofa, a desk, a chair, a coffeemaker, and a small fridge. Though Herb kept justifying the office, telling her why it would allow them more quality time together, Pippa was actually relieved to have him out of the house a bit. She wasn't used to their new constant proximity, and she felt the need to be by herself these days. Since she'd discovered the cigarettes on the car floor, flashes of apprehension would surge through her body out of the blue, like electric current. She was having alarming dreams. In one, a body was carried out of her neighbor's house on a stretcher. Someone unzipped the body bag, and it was Pippa, her face gray. In the dream, she wasn't actually dead, but she wasn't able to open her eyes or speak. As they carried her away, she realized with horror that she'd be buried alive. She didn't mention the dream to Herb. She didn't tell him she had been smoking, either. Every time she was about to mention it, as a sort of joke, she felt ashamed.

*

Pippa was just coming out of Why Not Furnishings in the mini-mall, carrying an almond-colored throw for Herb's new couch in an oversize shopping bag, when she heard a squeal of brakes, the heartrending scream of an animal, and the sickening crash of a car. She stood on her toes, craning her neck to see the road, then walked toward it uneasily. When she arrived, she saw that a tan Toyota had smacked into a lamppost. Its front end was crumpled. The driver, a man in his seventies, unhurt but dazed, was opening his door. A few old people were already clustered on the sidewalk outside the convenience store. Pippa walked toward them, made her way to the front of the crowd. There was Chris Nadeau, kneeling on the sidewalk, cradling a big white dog. The animal had a glistening, six-inch gash along its side. It was yelping. Chris was stroking its long white fur. When he saw Pippa, he looked up at her with such naked, beseeching sadness that she dropped to her knees beside him, then instantly regretted it. It was too intimate a thing to do. And now she was stuck there, crouched beside Dot's half-baked son, a dying dog in his lap.

'Is he yours?' she asked. He shook his head, looking down at the dying creature. 'I saw it happen through the window,' he said softly. She looked at the dog. It was whimpering and shaking. She found it unbearable to watch. She turned to Chris. He kept his eyes on the dog's face. The man who had hit the dog kept insisting, 'He jumped right out at me.' The dog started panting, its clear, light eyes fixed, white froth like whipped-up egg whites foaming at the corners of its mouth. Chris bent over and murmured something into its ear. Pippa couldn't see the dog, just the back of Chris's head. When he sat up, the dog was still, its eyes clouded over. Chris still didn't move. Neither did Pippa. They sat there, heads bowed, as though it was their pet that had died.

A van arrived with 'ASPCA' written on the side. Two men got out. Chris let them lift the body off him, then, without glancing at Pippa, he stood up and walked back into the convenience store.

One of the men from the ASPCA asked her if it was her dog. Pippa shook her head, brushed off her knees, picked up her shopping bag, and walked unsteadily to her car. She felt shaken and strangely moved.

*

Moira was late. Pippa leaned back in the aqua leatherette banquette and scrutinized the small oil paintings which were hung at regular intervals on the walls of the restaurant. They were all dutifully painted, humorless landscapes. She thought about her old friend Jim, how he would have looked up at them, his head slightly bowed. He would have nodded slowly. 'Ah, yes,' he would have said, smiling grimly. She wondered if Jim was still alive.

Moira appeared, out of breath, kissed Pippa, strands of black hair escaping from her ponytail. She smelled pleasantly of milk.

'I am so sorry I'm late, I was writing and I looked at the clock and –'

'Don't worry,' said Pippa, 'I was just relaxing, enjoying the art. That's a great buckle,' she said, fingering a silver sheriff star below Moira's belly button.

'Thanks,' said Moira, covering it with her hand and sliding into the opposite bench, her large suede handbag clutched to her side. An effeminate waiter appeared. 'Oh! Hi! Can I please have, um, an iced tea? The one with, um, melon in it?' Moira said to him with involuntary flirtatiousness. Then she looked back at Pippa, tucked a strand of hair behind her ear girlishly, and smiled, a dimple indenting her left cheek. No wonder she had been her father's favorite of seven kids, Pippa thought. She must have been a magical child, with that heart-shaped face, those enormous, Indian orphan eyes – and that imagination. In her messy, breathless, self-obsessed way, Moira was adorable. There was no getting around it. You could think her sincerity was ridiculous, you could lampoon her overblown sexuality, her exaggerated appreciation of life, but finally, you just had to throw up your hands and love the absolute purity of her confusion. Disarming. That was the word for Moira.

'You look *so beautiful*,' Moira said, scrutinizing Pippa's face. 'What are you doing different?'

'It's the indolence,' said Pippa.

'I wish I could be so peaceful and good like you.'

'*Good?*'

'You seem so . . . beatific.'

Pippa laughed. 'If only you knew.'

'Knew what?'

'Oh, a variety of things. I'm like one of those shiny used cars that have been in a terrible accident. They look perfectly fine on the outside, but the axle is bent.'

Moira smiled, puzzled. 'You're so mysterious about the past.'

'You think?'

'You never say anything about your life before.'

'There are things that happened that I don't dwell on.'

'What, like what happened to Herb's first wife?'

'Second.'

'Second. He said she was already crazy.'

'Not that crazy.'

Moira sighed, put her head in her hands, and sniffed.

'What?' Pippa put her palm on Moira's shoulder.

'I'm just a rotten apple,' said Moira, wiping the tears off her cheeks. 'I'll never have a normal life.'

Pippa was used to her friend's sudden episodes of self-flagellation. She always used humor to bring her out of her maudlin spirals.

'Oh, come on,' said Pippa. 'What's normal? You mean marriage?'

Moira nodded, blowing her nose. 'It's over between Sam and me. Oh, Pippa, it's all so completely fucked up. I – I've gotten myself into – I'm going to be forty with no man, fifty, not that it matters but it *does*. I – I just wish I knew how to recognize the right man.'

'Oh, pish tush,' said Pippa. 'You can be married to anybody, if that's what you're worried about.'

'What do you mean?'

'Pick any man in this room, in the right age range, I could be married to him.'

Cheered up by the game, Moira surveyed the room, then pointed to a thin man wearing glasses, looking at the menu with distaste.

'He just needs his routines, that's all,' Pippa said. 'I bet you if you anticipate his needs before he knows he has them, he'll be docile as a lamb.'

'What about that one?'

'As long as you stick your finger up his ass when he's coming, he won't give you any trouble at all.'

'Pippa!'

'Sorry, it just slipped out.'

'You make it seem like . . . so unromantic.'

'Courtship is romantic. Marriage . . . is an act of will,' said Pippa, taking a sip of water. 'I mean, I adore Herb. But the marriage functions because we will it to. If you leave love to hold everything together, you can forget it. Love comes and goes with the breeze, minute by minute.'

Moira shook her head, smiling, baffled. 'I can't get my head around that one,' she said.

'You'll see,' said Pippa, amazed at this act of complacent cynicism she was playing. When in God's name had she started saying 'pish tush'? When had she even heard it? Did she really believe what she was saying, about marriage being an act of will? Yes, she realized sadly, she did. After all she and Herb had been through together, after what they had lost to be with each other – their very souls, perhaps – being married ended up being *an act of will*. It made her want to tear through the dull present, claw the vivid past back into herself, devour it like a bear busting into a camper's stores. She wanted to run out of the restaurant, to find Herb and kiss him violently on the mouth (she could imagine his surprised, bemused expression as she crushed herself on him), to burst into tears, scream even – lose control at last. Instead she waited, smiling, for her lobster sandwich, and wondered if she might be on the brink of a very quiet nervous breakdown.

Part Two

Pippa Begins

I emerged from Suky's womb fulsome and alert, fat as a six-month-old, and covered in fine, black fur. After a brief look round the delivery room, I turned my face to my mother's swollen little dug and latched on, sucking so noisily that I sounded like a litter of piglets. My mother burst into tears at the thought of having given birth to this beast. The doctor's reassurances that I had merely been gestating a little too long, and thus had time to grow a dusting of vestigial hair, harkening back to the days when human beings belonged to the ape family, did nothing to calm her down. Being the wife of a pastor, she was ambivalent about evolutionary theory, and couldn't help feeling that my bestial looks, explicable as they apparently were by science, somehow reflected a basic flaw or sinfulness in her own character. Handing me back to the flabbergasted doctor, she launched herself off the delivery table, her legs still rubbery from the anesthetic, and ran down the hall, slipping on her own blood and screaming '*I had a monkey!*'

It took two nurses and a doctor to subdue all five feet, two inches of Suky Sarkissian. They injected her with a sedative, then gave her a private room, which our insurance didn't cover, but the hospital threw in for free.

*

The sense that her daughter magically embodied all that was wrong in herself never left my mother. Long after I had lost my furry coat and grown into a pretty, chubby little girl, she thought she discerned in me a deviousness, a lustiness, a general *badness*, which was, in secret fact, her own. At the age of two, I would clamp myself to her leg like an amorous dog. She always shook me off her, shrieking. One time, desperate to be freed from a crowded Greyhound bus, I scratched her face until it bled. She wept for my cruelty. I even took a crafty little poop in one of her favorite shoes, hoping to foil her plan of going out to dinner one night. It was one of a pair covered in pink velvet that matched her new dress perfectly. When she saw what I had done, she tried to be furious, but she couldn't stop laughing. For, in spite of the flaws in my character, or because of them perhaps, Suky loved me fervently, even ardently. She just couldn't get enough of me, couldn't stop cuddling, sniffing, kissing, nipping at me. I remember at the age of six or seven struggling to emerge from one of her embraces, not because I did not enjoy her affection but because I actually could not breathe.

I was the first girl after four boys. Suky mothered my predecessors fine; she herded them into and out of the bath as if it were a sheep dip, then shooed them into bed like a flock of pigeons. She ferried them conscientiously to their endless sports competitions. Yet I had the feeling, growing up, that Suky saw only me. Being the only girl, I had my own bath every night, and Suky would sit on the lid of the toilet, legs crossed, languorously watching me as she filed her nails, or stood at the mirror plucking her eyebrows. We would chat about this and that – the other girls in my school, who was friends with whom, who was planning on running away, what hairdo was best for which occasion – while in the next room my brothers shouted and teased and bashed one another over the head. At bedtime, she gave all the boys a swift kiss good night, but she lay down with me, tenderly stroking my head till I was asleep. We would dance to Bobby Darin in the kitchen, my feet on hers, holding hands, round and round and round.

I was the youngest, and for a few years, this lavishing of attention made a certain amount of sense. But once I was six and could fend for myself, the boys began to resent Suky's clear preference for her only girl. She even bought a camera, the sole function of which was to take pictures of me. She dressed me as angels, cowgirls, movie stars. Occasionally she photographed me naked. She was the most passionate of mothers.

Suky was a diminutive, peppy woman with bright red hair and a high, squeaky voice with a slight southern lilt, a shadow of her mother's viscous Mississippi drawl. Her waist was so tiny, her ankles so slim, she had to shop in the teen section of the local department store. I was proud of Suky's Tinker Bell figure; other people's mothers, with their rounded, fleshy bottoms and jiggling breasts, struck me as bovine and sloppy compared to my lithe, lively, tireless mother.

Suky smiled easily, wore her hair in a low beehive, and nearly always kept her eyebrows up in an expression of bemused surprise. In spite of this, I think she was a closet pessimist. I could tell by her driving. As she maneuvered our fat-assed station wagon around the narrow country roads, she sat bolt upright, her little hands clamped to the steering wheel, knuckles white. Every time we approached a turn, she whacked the horn, warning the eighteen-wheeler that was surely barreling round the bend, making ready to spin out of control and flatten us. An insomniac, she would stay up deep into the night, baking cookies, paying bills, or just pottering around. I remember waking from a bad dream in the middle of the night. The house was dead quiet. Knowing she'd be up, I walked downstairs and found her trimming the dead leaves off the plants in her pajamas. She was happy to see me. She made cocoa; we snuggled up to each other and watched TV till five, when we both passed out on the sofa, her arms around me, my head on her breast.

Suky slept there often. She'd say she was up so late, there was no point going to bed. We'd come down and find her huddled under the blanket she kept for watching TV. I would shake her awake, and she'd shuffle into the kitchen, drink a glass of orange juice, look at the clock. At seven on the dot, she'd take her medication – she was always muttering about her thyroid being off-kilter. By the time my dad came downstairs, she was dressed and cheerful, masterfully fixing everyone's breakfast, packing lunches, organizing book bags. She cooked nourishing meals but rarely sat with us at the table for long, preferring to stand by the stove spooning rice pudding from a china cup into her endlessly chattering mouth.

But then there were days when my chirpy, talkative, cheerful mother went quiet and staring, seemingly deaf to even my requests. She would dump the dinner on the table and rush away from the teeming mass of us to lie down and eat toast with butter in front of the television that stood at the foot of her bed. My father, Des, sighed when this happened, but he didn't reproach her. He knew there were times when his wife quite simply shorted out, went limp and affectless as a run-down robot. Des would rally then; singing in his painful rasp, he washed dishes, supervised baths. I relished these evenings being overseen by my father, because he would ignore me a little. I was just part of the other kids, not a unique and special creature, not the apple of anyone's eye. It was a relief. I roughed around with the boys, wrestled, kicked, giggled. But inevitably a sense of guilt overwhelmed me on those nights and, wish as I might to simply go to bed with a rough kiss from Dad, skipping the elaborate affections of my mother, I felt her pull me toward her; her will had infested my own. I walked into her room then. She was always fully dressed, on the bed, her plate of toast on her abdomen. She looked at me with a mix of joy and apprehension, as though at any moment I might renege on my affections. I had such power over Suky; it frightened me and made me bold. Sometimes I let my face go cold and stony just to watch the fear flash in her eyes.

Des

An impassive Hartford Armenian, my father had a thick, gravelly voice that made him sound as if he had just eaten a large spoonful of peanut butter. He moved his powerful, squat body with a deliberate, oxlike slowness. The russet circles surrounding his kind black eyes made him look perpetually exhausted. Father Sarkissian never got too happy, but then he never got too sad, either. His unlikely choice to become an Episcopalian minister had been made against the wishes of my grandfather, a fervent Armenian Orthodox who never forgave his Protestant wife for luring their only son from the church of his ancestors.

As it turned out, Des was a born pastor. He worked on his sermons scrupulously, kept the rectory open late for lost souls who needed a sympathetic ear. Yet one sensed, beneath the folds of his holy robes, not the airy, bodiless expanse of the spiritual man but the squirming flesh of a man all too much alive. Des always emphasized Christ the man in his sermons, to the point that some of his parishioners wondered aloud whether he actually thought Christ was also God, seeing as he nearly never mentioned it. To be honest, I don't think my father cared much about the God part. The miracle was the reality of Christ, his it-ness, the *fact* of him. I remember at dinner he once said that what really mattered was what people did to each other here on earth. The Holy Ghost could take care of itself.

Des was a compassionate man. He listened with a concerned, interested look as people with porridge-colored complexions and red-rimmed eyes told him their troubles on their way out of church or at our house in the evenings, when they had put their children to bed and had a few hours' respite before their daily obligations kicked in again. He seemed to enjoy us kids, in an abstracted sort of way, cocking his head and watching us as we did our homework, argued, played. He was always tender with us when we were hurt or sad and would sit with a weeping child for an hour, well after the crisis had passed, holding a small hand, in no rush to go anywhere. In that sense, he was the opposite of Suky, who skittered around in a flurry of activity eighteen hours a day. She relaxed only when she lay down with me to put me to sleep, humming wisps of songs into my ear in her high, breathy voice and curling a strand of my hair round her finger.

The truth is, I never got to know my father very well. Suky eclipsed him; the fire that burned in her day and night blotted him out in my imagination. He was a shadow figure, a refuge at times but not fully real to me as a man. I find this sad, because now I realize that, of all my traits, the ones I got from my father are the most valuable; it was the Des in me that allowed me to survive.

It didn't seem strange to me that my parents barely spoke to each other. Their exchanges were almost entirely confined to talking about the children, or simple requests, such as 'pass the milk please.' As far as I could tell, Suky spent any free time she had with me. She got most of her affection from me, too. I wonder what my parents' life together was like before I was born, or when they were newlyweds. In one early photograph, they seem shyly happy together, holding hands and smiling outside my father's first parish in Hartford. My mother is wearing a flowered housedress. Her face is young and round. Growing up, I was fascinated by this image, because Suky was not tiny then. She was almost plump.

Dolls and Husbands

I was always a housewife when I played, a little mother pushing my toy vacuum cleaner, a fussily dressed baby doll on my hip, or primly taking messages on a pink pretend phone for my husband, a tall, shadowy being I called Joey. Sex with Joey was a swift, choreographed movement. I would lie down, flap my legs open and closed, and stand up again, returning to my chores. I think I got the idea that you lie down from my friend Amy, who was, at nine, already a bit of an aficionado.

'You know what the worst word in the world is?' Amy asked me one day as we played in the dark corridor of our second floor. 'What?' I asked. Amy stood against the window, pensively swiveling the head of one of my dolls round and round. A web of fine, shiny brown hair tumbled to my best friend's waist. Her cornflower blue, crescent-shaped eyes gave her an old-fashioned, wistful air. 'Fuck,' she said flatly. Then she turned to look across the street at her older brother, Andy, who was mowing the town green. Amy's family was rich compared with ours, yet all the kids but Amy had summer jobs, to teach them the value of money. I watched Amy from behind: her arms rested on the crossbar of the window frame. Her lilac dress was cinched at the waist by a slender belt and fell in neat little pleats to just below her knees. Her bare feet were crossed at the ankles. I felt awed by her elegance and her beauty. There had never been such a girl, I thought, so perfect, so confident, so lovely. I felt like a troll in comparison. I was short, my face was flat, my hair was the color of straw, my eyes like gray marbles. One summer afternoon, as I pulled on my bikini bottom, Amy contemplated my muscular stomach with a cool, thoughtful air.

There was a faint line on my belly, like a sepia seam, from my navel to my sex. She pointed to it and said, 'You know what that means, don't you?'

'What?' I asked.

'When you were in your mother's stomach, you were going to be a boy until the *very last second*.' I looked in the mirror, at the broad muscles in my little shoulders, the round, strong thighs. I didn't look like a girl at all.

'You're a boy-girl,' she said, laughing. I laughed, too, though I felt my throat constricting. I shoved her onto the bed, and we tumbled, hysterical now, screaming, wrestling. Then we lay very still beside each other, catching our breath. I propped myself up on one elbow. Amy had a chipped front tooth that glimmered inside her parted lips.

'If I'm a boy-girl, then I can be your boy-girlfriend,' I said.

'No you can't,' she said dismissively.

'That way, when you have a real boyfriend, it'll be easy.'

She mulled this over for a moment. 'But we wouldn't tell anybody.' She looked at me, her eyes narrowing.

'You think I'm dumb, or crazy?' I asked. Then I let myself tip forward, very slowly approaching her face, and kissed her. Her lips felt cool and rough. She pushed me away, laughing, but later that day she let me do it again.

We kissed a few more times that summer. I persuaded her to let me lie on top of her twice, as well. I loved feeling myself crush down on her. She struggled out from under me, though. Once, I was surprised to see alarm in her face as I pinned her down; she was clearly relieved when we heard my mother's steps on the stairs.

Years passed. Amy turned out to be a very intelligent girl. She got A's in everything but history, a subject she detested for some reason of her own. I was an indifferent student. The words in my schoolbooks held no reality for me. I consumed them reluctantly, as if they were stale bread. I spent less time with Amy now; she was always in the library with her brainy friends. She studied at a round table with those geeks, sitting up straight like a princess, her long, dark hair glistening down her back, and worked away for hours under the admiring gaze of Mrs Underwood, the wheezing librarian. Ravaged by cigarettes, she rolled an oxygen tank with her while she was stacking books.

The kisses Amy and I had shared melted away into a childhood we both remembered like a dream. I could no more have kissed her now than fly a 747. I wouldn't have known how. I was thirteen, and I must tell you I was really something. Two compact and perfectly formed breasts had sprung up on my chest like mushrooms, overnight it seemed, disconcerting my brothers and sending my mother on an emergency shopping trip for my first bra. It took my father months to notice them. I'll never forget the look of muted surprise on his face as I bent to clear his plate and he realized what had happened to me. I was small and lithe, with copper-colored hair, padded little hands, and a face like a cat. That's what everyone said, that I looked like a kitten, with my broad, flat face and wide, slanting gray eyes, my small, cupid's bow mouth – and my lassitude. I could lie on the couch in a torpor all morning long, then spring up and bolt out the door in a pair of tiny shorts, my mother shouting after me, pleading with me to come back in and change.

As I have mentioned, I was a sexual creature pretty much from the get-go. At eleven, I found a way to achieve orgasms while doing the breaststroke, which subsequently led me to join the swim team of my junior high school and accounted for my iron thighs. In my early teens, though virginal in the extreme – I had never even kissed a boy – I developed a peculiar fantasy in which I met a faceless, unimpeachable gentleman whose pristine heart was overwhelmed with forbidden love for me. The boys in my school held no interest for me. They were all dying for it. I needed to find someone who absolutely didn't want to be seduced. But I'm getting ahead of myself. At the moment, I'm thirteen, Grandma Sally has thrombosis, and Suky is going to Delaware.

Aha!

Grandma Sally was fat. We saw her as rarely as possible. Suky could hardly look her. But, thinking back on it now, I don't think it was disgust and embarrassment about Sally's weight that kept her sparrowlike daughter away from her. I think the reason was that Grandma Sally had the full measure of my mother. I remember, on one of her rare visits, Sally followed Suky with her hooded eyes as her daughter sped around the kitchen, sponged down the table, made individually tailored, assembly-line sandwiches for each of her children (none of whom liked the same things), then swept the floor – talking breathlessly all the while. The whites of the old lady's eyes glimmered beneath dark irises; her double chin was cradled in her hands, a half-eaten piece of pie on a plate between her elbows, two thin, blond braids pinned to the top of her head. Eventually, she sat back, crossed her arms over her chest, and drawled in pure Mississippian: 'You never moved that fast when you were a kid.'

'Well, Mother,' Suky said with forced cheer, gritting her teeth, 'when I was a kid, I didn't have five children.'

'You were a lazy, dreamy kid,' said Sally. 'Nobody changes their tempo that way. Tempo is tempo. It's one of the basic things about a person.'

'You and I just have different styles of mothering,' said Suky, smiling coldly and patting her stiff nest of hair. 'I like to keep on top of things, that's all.'

'Mmm-hmm,' said Sally suspiciously, shifting her enormous weight on her chair and poking at her pie with her fork. I couldn't figure out what Grandma Sally was getting at – but I knew it enraged my mother. Her anger made my belly tense up and ache.

71

The discomfort was so intense, I went outside, in order to break the suction between us.

But that December, Grandma Sally seemed to be dying, and in need of her hyperefficient daughter to play nurse. So off Suky went, having left enough soup and lasagna in the freezer chest to last us a month, even though she only planned to be gone four days. The first two days of my vacation from Suky were heavenly. I'd amble home from school with my brothers, stare into the refrigerator, poke around in the cabinets, eat whatever I felt like, turn on the TV. Des spent afternoons in his study, working on his Sunday sermon, or meeting troubled parishioners. One parishioner who seemed especially troubled that week was Mrs Herbert Orschler. I always thought of her whole name when I saw her, because she once dropped an envelope from her purse, and I picked it up. Before I handed it to her, I read, typed out, 'Mrs Herbert Orschler.' I thought what an odd name Herbert was for a woman and wondered if, nestled beneath her snug dress, was a small, secret penis. Amy, that fountain of information, had once told me there were people who were born both male and female. This disgusted and fascinated me, and I wondered whether Mrs Herbert Orschler was visiting my father so often because of the stress caused by her genitalia. The day after my mother left for Grandma Sally's, I was passing the door to Des's study. It was ajar; I peeked in to find Mrs Orschler seated in an armchair, my father leaning in to hold her hand. This seemed slightly odd to me at the time, but I put it down to the duties of a pastor, which were mysterious and manifold, as my father always said.

It turned out that Suky had to stay away a whole extra week tending to her mother, whose approach to death was as sluggish as her housekeeping. (She would in fact outlive Suky by five years.) Back in the rectory, benign neglect was the order of the day. I didn't do my homework once. We ordered in pizza nearly every night and ate it in front of the television, ignoring the laden freezer. I don't think I washed much. A pact had developed between us kids and our father: he wouldn't bother us if we didn't bother him.

The caramel colored plastic bottles of pills in Suky's bathroom medicine cabinet and nestled between the nutmeg and the cloves in the spice rack were just part of my childhood, part of the furniture, like the rough cotton drapes in the living room or the one chipped square of brown linoleum in the kitchen. I didn't think about the shiny capsules, one half blood maroon, the other a transparent little dome filled with cheerful red and yellow orbs like miniature gumballs, which my mother swallowed in the morning and the afternoon with a toss of her head, hand to mouth fast as a hummingbird, until I heard the word "Dexedrine" in a cautionary TV movie about speed-addicted beatniks I watched one rainy afternoon with my oldest brother, Chester. The word rang a bell. I stole into the kitchen and checked the prescription bottle. Sure enough, the active ingredient was Dexedrine. Speed! All at once, the manic cheerfulness, the jumpiness, the sudden bouts of deflated disconnection, Grandma Sally's suspicions – all started to make a horrible kind of sense. Even Suky's overwhelming affections seemed like drug-induced delirium. I took the bottle and ran into the living room. Chester was slumped on the couch, his long legs splayed out, a vacant look on his face as he watched TV. I showed him the label.

'Mom takes that stuff,' I said, gesturing to the television. He turned toward me slowly, irritated by the interruption.

'What are you doing with Mom's medicine?'

'It's Dexedrine. See?'

'So?'

'So that's why she's so perky all the time.'

'Oh, shut up. She's not a drug addict. Those people in the movie are taking it to get high.'

'But what's the difference?'

73

'You think companies would sell diet pills full of speed? It's a tiny amount in there. I can't believe you're even saying this.'

I just stood there in front of him until he kicked me out of the way. Maybe he was right. Maybe she didn't need the pills except for a diet. So I took ten of them, just to see.

Whoosh! *Wow* did I have energy! I jumped up and down on my bed for about half an hour, my heart racing, then I ran downstairs and started telling Chester all these really funny things, and imitating our neighbors, and laughing, falling over myself. Des even came out of his study; I was absolutely nuts.

'What the heck happened to her?' he asked.

'I'll bet you she took Mom's diet pills,' said Chester sleepily. 'She was asking about them.'

'Why didn't you tell me?' Des asked, springing into action. He grabbed me by the arms and pinned me down on the sofa, under the light.

'Open up your eyes!' he commanded. I couldn't stop laughing.

'Goddamnit, open your eyes!' He held my eyelid open. I saw his tawny face, with the bluish cast of his shaved beard under the skin, his bushy eyebrows, the dark hairs escaping from his nose, so close it was alarming. 'We're going to have to take her to the hospital,' he said. I slipped out of his grasp, bolted up the stairs, dove into my room, and locked the door. Then I huddled in the corner, my mind going off like fireworks, my legs twitching. They had to pick the lock. In the end, Des decided against the hospital. I was coming down anyway, and had already started crying and throwing up.

I woke up at 9:30 the next morning. The house was silent. I came down to find Des, sitting in front of a cup of tea and the paper. He smiled at me kindly. I basked in his focused gaze.

'Sleep well?' he asked.

'How come you didn't wake me up for school?' I asked.

'Your body needed the rest, after yesterday. That was a dangerous thing you did.'

'If those pills are dangerous, why does Mommy take them?'

'They're not dangerous for her, she takes just a few, and she's a grown-up, not a kid.'

'But why does she take them?'

'Her mother got so terribly fat,' said Des. 'She's afraid the same thing will happen to her.'

'Is she . . . an *addict*?' I asked, using the word I'd learned from the TV drama.

'Oh, for mercy's sake, Pippa, sit down and eat your cereal. Your mother is no more an addict than . . . that squirrel out there.' I looked out the window. A large gray squirrel was frantically gnawing on a seed dropped from our bird feeder. The creature did, in fact, move a lot like Suky.

When I came home from school the next afternoon, Suky was in the bath. I barged in, opened the medicine cabinet, and took out the bottle of pills. I had two more bottles in my fist: one from the kitchen and another I had found behind the tomato paste in the larder. Suky glared at me, her face tight with anger as I lined up the bottles neatly, side by side.

'So who are you, really?' I asked. There was a long pause. 'I'd like to know what you're like without this stuff.'

'Don't be silly,' she said in a chilly, reasonable tone she almost never used with me. 'That is medicine. You took enough to kill you.'

'What would happen if you stopped taking it?'

'I would get fat,' she announced crisply, arching her back so her pink nipples peeked out of a skin of bubbles, then sank again.

'I don't care what you look like,' I said softly. She rested her feet on the end of the tub and assessed her glistening, pink toenails.

'Okay,' she said in an offhand way. 'Fine.' But she kept looking at her feet with stubborn interest until, eventually, I left.

The next day, the pills were gone. Not a pill in the house. That was her answer to me. She seemed more focused, serene, engaged. I was so relieved. The fact that she was wiping tears away while she was vacuuming and staring vacantly out the window while she ironed – my gratitude swept it out of my mind. At least she was my real mother. I loved her intensely then, and kept hugging her, kissing her. When I did, she smiled weakly and patted my arm. A week passed, and she started cheering up again. I never saw her take a pill, but she was acting like she'd drunk six cups of coffee, all day. I knew she must be hiding the drug somewhere. Whenever I got a chance, I searched. I found small stashes of pills in Baggies all over the house – in her underwear drawer, inside the freezer, taped under the couch. In the beginning, I would remove them and flush them down the toilet. But it didn't make any difference. She seemed to be taking more and more. Burying the habit had made it more important, the need more acute. Her behavior was erratic. Her pupils were constantly dilated, her reactions to sudden noises, even the telephone, were exaggerated, almost theatrical. She was prone to sudden bursts of weeping.

I tried to talk to Des about it again, but he brushed me off gruffly. They were in it together for some reason. And then I saw it – or I thought I did. With Suky out of her mind on speed, he was free to pursue the spiritual life, including consoling Mrs Orschler, and whomever else he had tucked under his robes of office. But now I think that was unfair. I think he was simply kind enough to accept Suky for who she was, and unwilling to have me insult her with a truth that could only be destructive. Or no. Maybe my father couldn't face that his wife was a drug addict because to face it would be to see his marriage and his life as a lie. So he didn't see it. Or maybe he was just plain lazy. I'll never know.

By the time I was fifteen I could barely look at Suky; her touch made my skin hurt. Each time I pulled away, she lowered her eyes, as if acknowledging her sin. I could see the glimmer of tears beneath her lids. I watched her behavior now with a coldly observant eye. She met my gaze with a strident stare. We had always known what the other was thinking, my mother and I. So, without having a single conversation, I expressed my disgust and sense of betrayal, and she, in her own way, refused to be controlled. Dinners became unbearable. She would prattle on senselessly from her station by the stove, laughing and blushing or crying and crazy, and I would stare at her, fantasizing about smacking her in the head, till I couldn't take it anymore and had to go into the bathroom, sob, and hit myself in the face. Returning glassy-eyed to the table, I would find my father and brothers eating and exchanging monosyllables, passing the dinner rolls as if nothing was the matter. Suky and I were on our own, locked cheek to cheek, dancing jerkily to a long, long number.

And Another Thing

When I was little, I had a bottle, of course, the way everyone does. Suky loved giving me my bottle. I kept it for a long time. When I turned three, four, she still made me a bottle with warm milk, or juice. And it didn't end there. When I was eleven, twelve, if Suky felt especially warmly toward me, or we'd had a fight, she would offer me a bottle. And I loved it. She would fix it for me, and I would lie down and drink, staring out the window like an infant. Even after I figured out about the pills, even once her touch made my skin ache and I had begun to daydream about her death, we could still make up with a bottle. The last one I drank, I was sixteen years old.

Good

By high school, I was angry, and that made me cool. Flanked by a few minions, I terrorized the kids that got on my nerves. Even Amy came under attack eventually. Little Miss Goody Two-Shoes was so pretty, you could eat her. She had the posture of a ballerina, carried her books level in front of her, like they were a chocolate cake. Needless to say, we moved in different circles now. But one day, as I watched her waft out of the girls' room, head held high, it occurred to me that she might tell one of her honor roll friends about our brief trip to the isle of Lesbos. If that got out, I would be ruined. I was seized by an impulse to smash her like a bug. I walked up to her and pinned her against the puce concrete-block wall, my hands squeezing her delicate wrists.

'If you ever tell anyone about us, I will beat you up,' I hissed. Amy's blue eyes widened; she looked from side to side for help.

'I won't,' she said. 'I promise. Please.' I let her go. She ran off. Tears stung my eyes. What the hell did I do that for? I loved Amy. I promised myself that the next day in assembly I would tell her I was sorry. But I was too embarrassed. And the worst of it was, after that day, Amy started fawning on me. She wanted me to be nice to her. She was lying down like a dog, letting me know I had won. She was weak and smart and beautiful and had a future, and I was strong and stupid and wasn't good at anything but scaring people. She would come up to me and make a lame joke, and I would smile with one side of my mouth, letting just a little air out of my nose. Once, I trapped her in one of the big gym lockers. I got a few of my henchwomen to circle her, and we shoved her in. She was screaming, pounding on the metal. My heart was slamming against my chest, I thought I was going to

81

faint. Afterward, she was angry, but she didn't stand up to me. She just walked away, sniffling.

Horrified at this bully I was becoming, I went to church every Sunday at nine o'clock and prayed to be a better person. My father's gruff, clotted voice ground on like a distant engine as my thoughts kneaded my sins over and over, turning them in my mind like dough. *Please, Jesus, come into my heart and change me I am begging you I am begging you to make me good, please.*

One summer night, it was so hot, my open window was like the yawning mouth of a dead man, emitting no puff of air. It felt like the oxygen had been sealed out of the world. I slept fitfully, my hair wet with perspiration, my legs flung over the sheets. Every few minutes, it seemed, I woke and looked around me, hoping for the dawn. The night-light emitted a sickly green glow. Each time I woke, I lay and listened to the tree frogs: ribbons of high-pitched sound layered on top of one another to create one pulsating scream that reached into my dreams like a claw, dragging me, time and again, into my room and the heat.

I heard a sound, a fluttering, thudding sound, coming from the open window. A flash of white, and then a clumsy thing, a feathered, heavy animal fell onto my floor and waddled toward me, its belly brushing the carpet. I wanted to scream, but I could not. Its webbed feet and large wings dragged along the floor, as if it was unused to perambulation. It twisted its neck to look up at me, and I saw a broad, solemn, human face, the face of a fifteen-year-old boy. The thing had shapely arms, too, which grew from the feathered trunk. With a sudden, violent flapping of wings, it heaved itself aloft and landed on my bed, its rubbery, black-skinned paddles scrambling over my bare feet. I crept back, terrified and repulsed, shrinking into the corner. The creature settled onto my crumpled bedclothes like a broody hen, then looked at me, somewhat out of breath from its efforts. It had pale, light-soaked eyes. I knew it for an angel, yet it disgusted me. I wondered if I had invoked it with all that praying I'd been doing.

'I'm sorry,' I whispered. That seemed to cover everything – both the bad behavior and the excessive prayer. The great wings began to spread; the thing extended itself, stood up; it was the height of a small man, towering over me in that bed. The wings were as wide as a canopy above me. One pale, human arm floated down toward me. I felt its hot hand resting on my head. My eyes were so heavy, I strained to keep them open; the eyelids felt glued together. The thing's hand was hot, burning; heat surged through my body, then it felt like tiny insects were crawling inside my skin. When the feeling receded, my eyes snapped open. The angel had vanished. I looked around me, frightened, breathless, ran to the open window, shut it, locked it.

The next morning, I was running a fever. My mother kept me in bed. I wondered what she would think of my angel. Would she believe he was real, and if so, what would his visit signify to her? She would probably think there was something unseemly about it. Suky had a dirty mind. She always leapt to salacious conclusions, about parishioners, politicians, movie stars, using amused disapproval to mask intense interest in anything sexual. Why would my angel be any different? I yearned to tell her, but I was afraid, because I knew she would see my angel as her fault, somehow. My sins were her sins; I was a part of her. That was the way she saw it.

Mr Brown

I sat through a lifetime of Sunday mornings, and in all that time I can remember only one of my father's sermons. I don't know if that is because it was so beautiful or because my father gave it to the congregation on the very day that changed my life. I was sitting in my usual seat in the front row, to Suky's right. She sat bolt upright, her eyes pinned to my father, eyebrows up, her small, weathered hands clamped together, one foot jiggling as my sleepy brothers slumped, inert, on the other side of her.

The sermon was about the cross, and how it is made up of both a vertical and a horizontal beam. Christ, my father posited in his growling voice, was those two things: vertical – godly – and horizontal – of the earth, a living creature. Christianity existed where the two lines met. He said that was what was so special about our God. He had been one of us, yet he was endless and almighty. Because I was actually listening to him for once, I truly saw Des at that moment. He was not a tall man. The way he held his short arms out as he described the cross, palms up, as if feeling for drops of rain in a drought, made him seem futile and precious – a man praying for order in a life governed by chaos. I felt so sorry for him. And then I turned, and it happened. I laid eyes on Mr Brown.

He was sitting across the aisle from me and one row back, beside the Oakley boys, boarders from the local boys' prep school, in their maroon blazers with light blue crests on the pockets and wrinkled navy slacks. The campus, with its white clapboard buildings and dark green shutters, was, in fact, only a stone's throw away from my house, across the green. From the first moment, I couldn't keep my eyes off Mr Brown. He was in his forties and seemed ancient to me at that time. But there was something about his face – a bony, veined face – that seemed deeply *good* to me. I loved his rust-colored mustache, his balding pate, his ruddy cheeks. Every Sunday after that, I situated myself in a place where I could see him; I even sat right next to him for one thrilling service. All my life till then, Suky had sat to my left at church. Once I started moving around, she was puzzled, but she didn't stop me. She rarely disciplined me anymore; when she tried, I shrugged her off with a poisonous glare.

Mr Brown always looked straight ahead during the service, like a bird dog. His wife was an athletic-looking, serious woman. She seemed preoccupied all the time, never speaking to her husband, and acting as if he wasn't beside her at all. He compulsively stroked her shoulder with his thumb, his arm around her, and occasionally he would whisper something in her ear, which she would listen to, an opaque expression on her face, and nod. I became convinced that she didn't love him. I watched Mr Brown in church for ten months. He was my Unimpeachable Gentleman.

I got an after-school job at the Oakley Academy, working in the kitchen, just so I could be close to him. Every day at four o'clock, I would walk across the green to the enormous, steamy Oakley kitchen, reluctantly tuck my copper locks into the requisite paper bonnet, and start peeling carrots and potatoes, dicing celery, getting everything ready for the evening meal. Then it was showtime; I would serve the kids their grub. At first I was frustrated; all the contact I had with my beloved was saying hello as I spooned mashed potato and meat loaf onto his plate. But I shot him glances as I worked. He ate with his wife every night. Their conversations seemed strained yet civil. He always pulled her chair out for her. He talked more than she did; mostly she nodded, unsmiling, staring into her plate. Directly after she had finished her meal, she stood up, murmured a goodbye, and walked out. Mr Brown would then get himself a cup of coffee and circulate around the dining hall, chatting with the boys. He seemed to relax when his wife was out of the room. He loosened his tie and sat at the edges of the refectory tables, joking with the students. He was reassuring with one, ruffled another's hair, spoke with stiff severity to another. I managed to catch his eye once or twice, but after several weeks I couldn't take it anymore. I had to speak to him.

One night, as he was walking down the hallway after dinner, I threw myself down a short flight of stairs and landed at his feet. I actually sprained my ankle doing this stunt, and he had to hold me up as I limped to the school infirmary. He smelled like talcum powder. At one point, my lip brushed his ear as I hobbled along. He blushed from his neck all the way up to his temples. That's when I knew I was getting somewhere. After that, he called me by my name and always asked how I was when I handed him his dinner. A couple of times I thought I noticed him lingering outside when I came out after my shift. But all he ever did was say 'hello' in a cordial, distanced way. Mr Brown was unimpeachable.

One night, as I left my job, my eyes dried up from exhaustion, my hands raw from chopping, I saw him walking up the stone steps to the dining hall, taking them two at a time with his long strides. He was about to pass me with a friendly greeting when I burst into tears. There was snot coming out of my nose, my knees went weak. I had to sit down. Mr Brown took out his handkerchief and sat down beside me. I wiped my nose and put my head between my knees. I was so embarrassed, but I was in heaven, too, because I could feel the palm of his hand on the small of my back.

'What is it, Pippa?' he asked. 'What's wrong?'

'I think I'm just tired.'

'You must be. It seems like a lot for a girl your age, a job after school. Are you sure it's necessary?'

'It's necessary,' I said.

'Can't you talk to your parents, maybe they can –'

'It's not the money,' I said. 'I mean, we don't have much money, but I don't have to have a job in the school year.'

'Then quit,' said Mr Brown. 'It's too much for you. Use the time to study, or be just a kid.'

'I can't quit.'

'Why not?' I shook my head then, looking around at the boys walking back to their dorms. One sped by us on his way down the stairs.

'Come with me,' said Mr Brown firmly. He led me by the arm to a building a hundred yards away. There were pillars on the front of it. He opened the door and guided me down a short hallway, reached into an open doorway, flicked on the fluorescent lights. It was a classroom with math equations written on the chalkboard. I followed him in and sat down. He sat on the desk in front of me.

'All right now. No one can hear you. Tell me what's wrong.' He was being the teacher now; he had done this countless times, led the troubled kid out of the herd for a few minutes of special time. I felt stupid to have thought it was anything else.

'It's nothing,' I said, looking up at him. 'I was just –' He was listening to me, but he looked so weary. I was about to give up on him, I really was, but then the tears came to my rescue. I felt them, hot and thick, trickling down my cheeks.

He hopped off the desk, squatted beside me and put his arm around the back of my chair. 'It's just . . . what?' he asked softly. I tried to think of a lie. I could tell him any horror now and he would believe me to be a victim of it. My mind was blank. I told the truth.

'If I quit my job, I wouldn't see you anymore.' There was a moment of silence. I looked right at him now. Telling the truth had made me powerful. I had nothing to lose. It couldn't get more embarrassing than this. He looked like the wind had been knocked out of him. And then his cheeks went all mottled. I loved the way his blood exposed him. That moment seemed to extend forever. I saw him hovering between falling toward me and retreat. I had to pull him in somehow. I had to take a risk. 'I love you,' I said. I knew immediately I had made a mistake.

His brows furrowed for a moment, then he sat back on his haunches. 'How old are you?' he asked.

'Sixteen and a half.'

'You can't love someone you don't know.'

'But I do know you. I've known you for almost a year. I watch you in church. I see you in the dining room. I know you're unhappy and lonely and blue, and that you don't feel loved. You've gotten used to nobody understanding you, nobody being curious about you. You're just Mr Brown, the guy who fixes things, just like you're here to fix me.' He looked up at me, pain and surprise on his face. 'You don't have to give me anything,' I said. 'I just . . . wanted you to know that there's someone who . . . sees you.' I felt his gaze churning into me. And I cannot describe how close to him I felt. Andrew Brown, dedicated teacher and resigned husband, was in a state of acute longing and desperation, and had become inured to that condition. But all it took was one little girl who really saw him and –

Mr Brown stood up, straightened his corduroys, and sniffed.

'You'd better go home now.' He smiled at me, a kind, sad, closed-lip smile.

'I'm sorry,' I said.

'Don't be, Pippa. Never be sorry for having feelings.' I walked out ahead of him and ran all the way home.

The next night, as I slid three slippery slices of turkey onto his plate and poured extra gravy over his mashed potatoes, I felt his eyes on me. I looked up, and there he was, his amber irises flecked with gold; the kindness radiated out of him. His wife came next. She looked right through me. The loose skin on her cheeks, her defeated, frowning mouth, seemed like an affront against the angelic Mr Brown. A week later, as I walked across the green at dusk after serving dinner at Oakley, I heard his voice. 'Pippa.' I turned. He was standing a few feet away. His breath was labored, as though he had hurried to follow me.

'Hi,' I said.

'Would you like to take a little walk?'

We walked into the sparse wood that fringed the green. The moon had risen, and mist hovered between the young trees. I faltered, stepping on a rotten log; Mr Brown took my hand. We emerged at the Depot. He let go.

The place was deserted. Pharmacy, liquor store, ice cream parlor – they looked like strange buildings I had never seen before. I was forbidden to walk through my town after dark. We walked to the end of River Road, then along the bank of the river. The moon shed cold, blue light on the faint track worn away by fishermen and kids looking for a place to smoke after school. I had come here myself on occasion. We walked along for a few yards, then he sat down on a big rock covered, I happened to know, with obscene graffiti.

We sat side by side for a few minutes, listening to the high gurgling of the little river. Mr Brown slid his soft, warm hand over mine. I looked at him. His face was mostly in shadow, but I could see his eyes. He looked so sad. I put my palm up to his face and left it there. And then, swiftly, without warning, the unimpeachable Mr Brown kissed me. His mustache was soft. The secret tongue inside it felt so warm and new; it was like licking a little, wet animal.

*

We were busted eleven months later, in the narrow attic room that Andrew Brown used as a study and a place to meet his students. We were half-dressed (Mr Brown never allowed us to be completely naked), intertwined and sated on the couch, gazing at a spider as it glided through the air from the ceiling on its own glistening filament, when the door opened with a cursory knock, then swiftly shut. We couldn't see who had come in, but Mr Brown immediately clamped his hands to his head, remembering his appointment with Mademoiselle Martel, a frowsy teacher visiting from Toulouse. And we hadn't locked the door!

I climbed down the fire escape, ran across the green to my house, and waited.

It turned out that, though French, Mlle Martel took a dim view of statutory rape. She blew the whistle, and my beloved Mr Brown was fired. I'm sure I was, too; I never went back to find out. My parents were called, however. Suky went hysterical. I mean really out of her mind. She wouldn't stop shaking. Tears were flying out of her eyes. She kept saying, 'How *could* you?' I leaned back on the wall and looked at her with false calm; behind my ribs, my heart was going berserk. Chester held her arms while my father popped a couple of sleeping pills into her mouth. I tried to laugh, but my throat was closing up.

I knew what was upsetting the pastor's wife. It wasn't her morals being tormented. It was jealousy, straight up. She was crazy with it. In fact, she was plain old crazy. They all were, really, my slow-moving, slow-talking brothers, with their laconic language and leaden eyes – they had all built their personalities up like bulwarks against her mania and neglect. Depressives, every last one of them. And my father – well, he had learned how to take care of himself. I had been eavesdropping on his phone conversations with Mrs Herbert Orschler for a year. The two of them met every Friday afternoon, like clockwork. Poor old Suky would have no lover now. Because I was leaving. I knew it the minute she heard the news; her face crumpled like a child who's lost her favorite teddy under the wheels of a bus. Gone forever, that little stuffed bear. I couldn't stay after that performance. I mean, I didn't need a degree in psychology to realize there was something wrong between me and my mother.

It came in handy that I was so pissed off. Not just by this one episode but by the pills, by her being so needy all the time – the whole thing. I had become like one of those men you see in the movies who wear aviator sunglasses and chew gum and never get ruffled. That's what I was trying to be: Clint Eastwood if he was a seventeen-year-old girl. I packed some clothes in a duffel bag, took my savings from the job at Oakley, drove my mother's car to the bus station, and left it there with the keys in it. I never got to say goodbye to Mr Brown. He left Oakley, without his wife. I never heard from him again, but years later I found out he was teaching at a school in Canada. I guess I sort of ruined his life. Or maybe I didn't. Maybe I just freed him from a miserable marriage and a pathetic, colorless existence. Maybe he's happy. Maybe he's got grandkids by now.

Aunt Trish

I knew Mylert Walgreen, the heavy, wheezing kid behind the counter at the bus station. He had graduated from my high school the year before. Mylert's curiosity was definitely piqued by my sudden, solitary trip to New York City in the middle of the school week. I had rarely spoken to Mylert in school; we traveled in different circles. He was one of the kids who shuffled through the halls, head down, knees rubbing together, hoping not to be noticed, not to be teased. I never bothered kids like that; I even defended them now and then against the other bullies. My prey was of a higher order: kids who thought they were cool but weren't. Mylert put on no such airs. Now that he'd graduated, however, he had a certain swagger, an air of adult authority that rankled me.

'Are you running away?' he asked.

'It's not your business what I'm doing, Mylert,' I said.

'I'm not supposed to sell tickets to unaccompanied minors,' he said.

I sighed, looking up at the ceiling, trying to gather my thoughts.

'So are you?' he asked. 'I won't tell anyone.'

'No, you dipshit, I'm going to visit my aunt Trish in New York. Now give me the ticket.'

'On a Wednesday?' I just glared at him till, looking somewhat put out, he took my money and officiously handed me the bus ticket. I was sweating. Aunt Trish. So that's where I was going. And now I had confided in Mylert Walgreen, of all people! My parents would find out within an hour. Oh, well. What was so terrible about that? I wasn't running away, I was moving away. I had no legal obligation to stay in school anymore. I was starting my life, and that was that.

As the bus pulled away, I thought of Mr Brown, his flared, delicate nostrils, the bewildered look that came into his eyes when he looked at me. I missed him so much.

*

Aunt Trish lived on Thirtieth Street and First Avenue, above the Fresh Day deli. I rang the bell marked 'Sarkissian'. The apartment was 45. I climbed five flights of wide brown metal stairs. The walls on the way up were lined with white ceramic tiles; the floors in the hallways were tiled with tiny, grimy black and white hexagons. The smell of cigarette smoke and fried onions mingled in the air.

After what seemed like half an hour, I found apartment 45. The door was ajar, and Aunt Trish was right behind it. A small woman, she was shorter than I was, but she gave me a bear hug that nearly cracked my ribs.

Aunt Trish was a kind, energetic, helpful woman. She wore round glasses, had short, dark hair; a constellation of black moles dotted her face. Her body was square, short, hunched forward, as though she were always getting ready to break out for a touchdown. I had called her from the bus station.

'Your father called before you did,' she said, crouching into a brown, nubbly couch with a Navajo blanket slung over the back of it. I fell into an armchair beside her, my legs spread wide. The chair had a high back and wings on either side of my head. 'Apparently, you told the boy at the bus station you were going to see your aunt Trish.' She grinned at this, showing the wide gap between her two front teeth.

'What . . . did my dad say?' I asked.

'He told me you got into trouble.'

'Did he say what kind of trouble?'

'Not exactly. Something about the prep school next door to you.'

'I fell in love with the math teacher. And we got caught. And my mom is a pill-head.' This last piece of news didn't seem to surprise Aunt Trish; it just made her go quiet, a sad smile on her face.

'So what's the plan, Stan?' she asked.

'I just don't want to live at home anymore.'

'You've only got a few more months of school left, right?'

'I'm dropping out.'

'You're gonna regret that.'

'All I know is, I'm not going home.'

Trish sighed and looked down at the mahogany coffee table for a long time. On it was a large book with a black-and-white photograph of a mountain on the cover. The scene looked cold and dreary. On the back wall of the living room was a colorful painting of mountains in a desert. There were cacti in the foreground; in the background, the sandy mountains were striped with pastel colors. I wondered what it was about mountains that Trish loved so much.

'Apparently, your mother is pretty upset,' she said.

'Oh, really?' Trish caught the ice in my gaze.

'Look, as far as I'm concerned, you can stay in – um – Kat's room for as long as you need to. You're my favorite niece, you know that. But there's going to be a discussion with your parents later today, and it's not going to be pretty.' Dread pulsed through me.

'They're coming?'

'They should be here in about two hours.' I felt trapped. Maybe the best thing was to get out while there was still time. But where would I go?

'Who's Kat?' I asked. Aunt Trish lit up a Marlboro from a pack in her shirt pocket.

'She's my roommate,' she said, inhaling.

'I didn't know you lived with someone.'

'She just moved in a couple of months ago,' said Aunt Trish. 'So. You hungry?' I shook my head. I hadn't eaten all day, but my stomach felt sealed. She was coming. Suky was coming. I had to hang on to this feeling of rage; I had to keep it going. If I let it collapse, if I let guilt creep in, I would end up in her arms; I would end up sucking on a baby bottle until I was twenty.

Eventually, the buzzer rang. My father's rasping voice sounded incomprehensible over the intercom. I worried about the two of them climbing all those stairs. Aunt Trish went into the hall and looked down the stairwell to be sure they found us. When they arrived, Suky looked wrung out, wan. She kept blinking really hard and smiling at Trish. Then she reached out to hug me and stopped her hands in midair. Des didn't bother taking his coat off. He sat down in Trish's wing-backed armchair and let out a long sigh. Suky and I were at either end of the couch. Trish stood leaning against the kitchen counter, a cigarette in the crook of her fingers, tilted forward, ready, as ever, for the big sprint. I couldn't believe Aunt Trish was even considering keeping me against the will of her older brother. She had always seemed so shy and easygoing to me. And in my experience, adults stuck together. But Trish was different. She rarely showed up for holidays or family gatherings. When she did, she always arrived alone and spent a lot of the time on our porch, on her own, smoking. She would call now and then, send cards and presents, but that was it.

'It's time to come home, Pippa,' Des said quietly.

'I'm not going home. I'm staying with Aunt Trish.'

Des looked at his sister darkly, then back at me. 'You can't just run away from what you've done,' he said. 'You can't do that in life.'

'I'm not running away,' I said. 'I'm just done, that's all.'

'What do you mean, you're done?' he said.

'I don't want to live . . . with you.' My eyes fell on Suky for a second, then away.

'Oh, so it's all my fault,' she said. Her voice sounded shrill, taunting.

'What's all your fault?'

'What you did. That man has been fired. His wife is, she is ... devastated.'

'I didn't say it was your fault. Nothing is your fault, okay? I just don't want to be home anymore. I can't go back there, and that's that. You can force me to go back, but I'll leave again. I'm done, don't you get it?'

Suky's eyes were swollen and overflowing. 'So you're not even coming home for Christmas anymore?'

'Mom, I didn't say that. Please. I will. Of course I'll come home for Christmas, I just don't want to live at home.'

'What did I do? What did I do to make you so secretive and unhappy?'

'Nothing. Please, Mom. Please.'

Des growled at Suky. 'Will you stop whipping her up? For mercy's sake.' Then, turning to me, he said, 'Do you realize your mother was so upset she had to get an injection to calm her down?'

I looked over at her. She looked crushed; her whole body was slumped to the side of the couch, her face a mask of misery and confusion. A muscle spasm dimpled her cheek with an irregular, spastic beat. I so wanted to make her better.

'Mommy –' I said. She brightened. A hopeful smile flickered on her face. 'I'm sorry, I – I just can't.' And then I got up and grabbed my coat from the peg in the entryway, flung open the heavy door, and clattered down the metal steps of Trish's building, my mother's voice echoing through the stairwell – 'Pippa come back – Pippa I promise –' I looked at her standing above me. Her stick-like body, that flame of hair: she was a lit match, burning herself right out. I don't remember what she promised. I ran away from her, down First Avenue, zigzagging thirty blocks downtown as the lights changed, all the way to Houston Street. I didn't know where I was going. I turned left and walked fast, head down, imagining her behind me, grabbing at my clothes. I passed Avenues

A, B, C, D, till I came to the East River. Then I just stood there on the side of the FDR Drive, cars whipping past behind me, and watched the boats go by, churning up water turned the color of fire by the setting sun's reflection. I was wearing a thin cotton peacoat, and the wind ripped through it. I turned up the collar, shoved my hands deep into my pockets.

'This is where I live' – I dared think it. Intense, surprising happiness socked me in the gut. No one knew exactly where I was at that precise moment. I was just another person in this vast city. If a truck swerved from the highway and mowed me down, I would go to the city morgue, be buried with the bums. For these few seconds, I had escaped the radar of my mother, my father, even Aunt Trish. I was just myself, connected to no one. I was free.

Shackles

When I got back to Trish's place, my parents were gone. I thought of Suky, of what she must have felt when I didn't come back. Of the long, silent car ride back home. I sat down on Trish's couch, put my hands over my face, tasted the salt of my tears.

Trish put her arm around me. 'Listen, kiddo. It's tough times. Your mom has a serious problem, okay? I'm saying it. I know no one else will. It's not your fault. I think you did right getting away. It doesn't mean it has to be forever. And it doesn't mean you can't call her and tell her you love her, either.' I started sobbing when she said that. Because I did love Suky. I loved her more than I could imagine loving anyone. I felt so bad for hurting her. Trish just kept her arms around me, saying, 'Sssh, ssh, it's not your fault. It's not your fault . . .' Eventually, she laid me down under the Navajo blanket and turned on the TV. *Gilda* was playing. I remember thinking, Rita Hayworth had red hair, Suky has red hair. And then I fell asleep.

When I woke up, it was dark outside the window, and I was immediately aware of two people whispering in the kitchen. I turned and saw a tall, gangly woman with dark hair the shape of a Roman centurion's helmet tossing salad in a bowl. She looked down at me and winked. 'Hey,' she said. Her voice was low, husky. Aunt Trish reached into the oven and took out a tray of sizzling beef patties.

I ate two hamburgers and drank a quart of milk. Kat and Aunt Trish watched me with indulgent grins on their faces. Kat had a lozenge-shaped face, a broad mouth, and eyes that slanted downward. Every now and then, she would bob her head to some song she had in her mind, humming very quietly to herself.

When I finally slowed down on the ravenous eating, Trish laid down the law. 'Okay, Pipps. Here's the deal I made with your parents. These are your choices.' She raised her stubby thumb. 'You go back to school here in the city.' The forefinger came up. 'You study on your own and take the high school equivalency test.' The middle finger now. 'You go back home.'

I opted for the test. No way was I going to negotiate another high school's social life for just one semester. It wasn't worth the stress. Kat stood up now, cleared the plates, then yawned, stretching her arms high so her concave belly showed beneath her short sweater. 'I'm gonna go work in my room a little, before Pippa goes to bed,' she said. 'Night, Pippa.'

'Night,' I said. Then Kat turned to Aunt Trish, bouncing from one foot to the other.

'See ya, baby,' she said, and bent down to kiss her. Trish moved her head so Kat had to peck her cheek, but Kat took her chin and held it, kissing her right on the mouth. All of a sudden I knew why Aunt Trish wasn't exactly a regular at family events. Kat skipped off into her room/my room. Trish looked at me and made a gesture, a that's-the-way-it-is-what-are-you-gonna-do shrug. I smiled at her encouragingly, raising my eyebrows.

'So we're a couple of black sheep, you and me,' said Trish. Then she cracked a smile and leaked a growling, phlegmy giggle. It was the nicest, most reassuring thing anyone had ever said to me. I felt I belonged somewhere. I belonged on the outside, with Aunt Trish.

*

Kat and Trish slept under a shiny maroon bedspread. Over their bed hung a large painting of a naked woman with huge eyes and very long eyelashes. She looked both cute and lewd. Life with Trish and Kat was quiet at first. Kat's room, where I was staying, wasn't a bedroom; it was an office with a couch in it. The desk was cluttered with papers and an electric typewriter. Though she worked as a secretary in a wholesale textile business in Chelsea, Kat was writing a novel. At six in the morning, she would glide in with a mug of tea that smelled of warm mud and start typing. I then dragged the comforter to the couch in the living room and tried to sleep until Trish stomped into the kitchen around seven. She worked in a warehouse in the meatpacking district, carried a clipboard.

Trish made me pull my weight: every day, I took out the garbage, cleaned the kitchen, mopped the floors, studied for the high school equivalency test. And looked for a job. I hadn't had much experience, aside from Oakley, and *they* weren't going to be giving me a recommendation anytime soon. Finally, I found a restaurant on the Lower East Side, El Corazón, willing to take a chance. I didn't speak Spanish and could barely make myself understood in the interview with the enormous, somber owner-chef, Señor Pardo. I couldn't see why they wanted an English-speaking girl working in the place at all till Señor Pardo pointed at a group at one table and said, 'You serve the English-speak customers.' I looked over. Three young men and a woman in their twenties huddled in a booth, speaking English and smoking filterless cigarettes. There was a pudgy, blond fellow with flecks of paint on his hands, an elegant, tall one with very long black hair, a girl with a large nose and an amused-looking, painted mouth, and a skinny guy with puffy eyes and a poker face who was slumped in his seat. They all looked exhausted. 'Now,' said Señor Pardo, handing me an order pad. I walked over to the group. 'The United States loses the war in Vietnam,' the pudgy one was saying, 'Greg Brady gets a perm.'

'Do you know what you want?' I asked.

'There goes the neighborhood,' said the thin, puffy-eyed fellow. But as he looked up at me with his poker face, his gaze stayed on me for an instant too long. They all ordered margaritas. I served this group almost daily for months, I learned their names, but I never went out with them, never saw where they lived. Until later.

*

I felt elated in Kat's presence. She was glamorous, in a way, always jutting out her small breasts, swiveling her narrow hips in tight bell-bottoms, making poor old Aunt Trish seem dusty and square, her dark eyes moist with devotion to the creature she shared her bed with. Once, I asked Kat what her novel was about. She flashed Trish a sly smile.

'Let's just say it's no work of art,' she said.

'But what's it about?'

'Love,' she said. 'The mysteries of love.' Aunt Trish blushed and got up to clear the table. I wanted to read that novel.

One night, the two of them had a dinner party. They invited a few women and two men. I was invited, too. I wore a lavender sundress, even though it was frigid outside. It was the only dress I had brought with me from home. When she saw me in it, Kat whistled a long, low note that made me blush. One of the women at the party was named Shelly. She was brash, had sandy blonde hair and a big chest. She kept saying, 'When I was in the film business,' which for some reason made everybody laugh except for Aunt Trish. She didn't laugh, she looked at her plate through her round glasses, smiling and shaking her head.

Then there was a man named Jim, small, in his forties, with yellowish skin, a handsome jawline, a cleft chin, and rotten teeth. He wore a felt fedora and an old tweed coat. He didn't drink the wine. 'I'm sick,' he explained to me in a breathy voice. 'So you and me will be sober, okay, and we can watch all the rest of them fall apart.' Jim was curious about me. 'So . . . where do you go to school?' I explained that I had dropped out, left home; I was on my own now. 'Very cool,' he said. 'Very unusual. You didn't run away. You left. I like the way you put that.' His watery, green eyes were constantly focused on another part of the room as he spoke to me, which made him seem blind, though I was pretty sure he wasn't. I asked him what his sickness was. He said he had diabetes. He'd already had to have a toe amputated. He removed his shoe, then his sock, and showed me a pale foot with a gap where the little toe was meant to be. 'And there are other . . . side effects I won't go into, which render me harmless,' he said, his lips turned up in a rueful smile. He was weird, but I liked him.

As the evening progressed, the heat from the radiators became so intense that people started taking off their cardigans, socks, stockings. Jim shed his coat and hat. His hair was very black. At one point, he leaned against the wall and left a smudge on it from the back of his head. The other guests were friends of Trish's: a drab, sad-looking couple of women who lived in New Jersey, and an acne-ridden man named Eric, who made flamboyant gestures, got very drunk, and had to lie down in the office. I hoped he wouldn't throw up in there. After the Boston cream pie, Kat shot up out of her seat. She was wearing a red, sleeveless dress that clung to her slender frame. 'I say we go out on the town,' she said, waving her long arms in the air like windmills, her cheeks flushed from the wine.

She turned to Shelly. 'You'd know where to go,' she said, jutting one hip out.

'I'm based in San Francisco now,' said Shelly. 'What do I know?'

'The city hasn't changed *that* much,' said Kat.

'What kind of an evening do you have in mind?'

'Insane,' Kat answered, winking at Aunt Trish.

Trish shook her head, smiling. She had work the next day; she wasn't going anyplace. She wanted to keep me home, too, but Kat insisted that I come along, with Jim as a chaperone.

'It's always handy to have a eunuch around,' said Jim as he hung Trish's parka over my bare shoulders.

I was happy to be going out for once, but I felt bad for Aunt Trish. She seemed so nervous. But she couldn't say no to Kat, not about anything. So we all tromped down the freezing street with our arms up, trying to flag down a cab. At last, two of them stopped for us and we divided ourselves up. The dreary women from New Jersey decided to get back on the PATH train, and the flamboyant man weaved his way uptown on foot. So I got into one cab with Jim, Kat, and Shelly. Shelly sat in the front. As we bounced downtown on no suspension, the chassis slamming the pavement with every pothole, Kat kept bursting into dance songs, punching her arms in the air like a boxer. Jim called out a few points of interest to me as we passed them: Fifth Avenue, the Flatiron Building, Union Square. We stopped on West Fourteenth Street, near the river. The street was deserted. The worn cobblestones shone with the light from a lone streetlamp. There was no sign of a club of any kind.

As if remembering something, Shelly turned to look at me, then started rummaging through her purse and took out a lipstick. 'We'll have to age her up,' she said, twisting up the shiny, red tube and applying some onto my mouth. Then she dragged my hair from its ponytail and ruffled it so it half-hid my face. 'Look,' she said to Kat. 'It's Veronica fuckin' Lake.' I felt Kat's eyes on me then, and I stood still for an extra second, my eyes averted, so she could see me as this Veronica Lake whom I had not heard of but I knew was beautiful. She had to be, with a name like that. Shelly beckoned to us. We followed her down a short, dark stairway, through a graffiti-scrawled metal door, to a ticket booth. The man behind the fingerprint-dappled Plexiglas seemed happy to see Shelly. His gray hair was greased back into a neat ducktail, his pockmarked skin the color of putty.

'Oh hi, Suzanne, where have you been?' he asked her in a nasal baritone.

'I'm based in San Francisco,' said Shelly.

'Welcome home. It's Ladies' Night! You've got one guy between the three of yous tonight? Ten dollars.' Jim reached for his wallet, but Shelly slid a crisp folded bill under the window. To our right was a fringed plastic sheet, like the kind in car washes. Hazy purple light shone behind it. Loud music throbbed. We ducked our heads and passed through this fringed hymen. Upon emerging,

I was amazed to see a middle-aged man wearing a fawn-colored turtleneck and glasses, naked from the waist down but for socks and running shoes. He had a drink in one hand, his half-risen penis in the other, and was masturbating halfheartedly, a bored expression on his face, while wandering around. 'Keep your back to the wall,' Jim suggested helpfully.

Sidling toward the edge of the room, I saw that it was lined with books. I moved closer to glance at the titles. They were all pornographic: *I Was a Teenage Sex Slave*, *Seven Amazing Fantasies Come True*. Several people were clustered around the spotlit center of the room, watching a man with a bushy mustache pour hot wax on a bound, pale woman's naked breasts. Her skin glowed in the light. A small, muscular fellow with a saddle strapped to his back trotted up to Shelly and greeted her effusively as Suzanne. Hand on hip, one leg thrust out, he asked her about a mutual friend, the leather of his tack creaking behind him. Shelly answered him with a slightly pompous affability; she was clearly a star of some kind in this netherworld. Meanwhile, Kat did a little solipsistic dance to the constant beat, occasionally throwing a few shadow punches. I tripped and fell, realizing too late that the bundle of dirty laundry I'd landed on was a scantily clad man chained to a metal pole. Jim hoisted me up with trembling arms as I apologized effusively. Just then, a petite woman being led on a leash by a skinny guy in a striped shirt came tottering up to Shelly, arms outstretched. We were all introduced. The girl had iron cuffs on her wrists, joined by a long chain. Her name was Renee; her boyfriend was Miles. Miles had a moist, boneless handshake. 'Sit,' he said to Renee. Renee sat down beside Shelly.

'How have you been?' she asked Shelly. 'The last time I saw you was in Chicago, at the leather conference.'

'Oh, God, that was wild.'

'I don't think we're going this year,' said Renee, widening her round, brown eyes and looking up at Miles complacently. 'Miles has a new baby nephew and he's being christened, so . . .' She crossed her legs. I realized then that her ankles were also shackled. Renee looked up at Miles again. 'Honey, could you get me a pop?'

'Sure,' said Miles. 'Anyone else want anything?' We shook our heads. He hesitated, holding the end of Renee's leash, unsure of whom to entrust it to. Finally, he settled on Jim.

'Will you hold this till I get back?'

'No problem,' said Jim, his serious face filled with submerged amusement.

'Pippa, are you in school?' asked Renee.

'I'm studying at home,' I said.

'I never even graduated,' she said.

'When did you . . . start –'

'Oh, this?' she said, raising her bound wrists, the chain tinkling. 'Um . . . we were both just kids, and one day we were making out in Miles's garage and he tied me up and we just really liked it!' Renee smiled, and deep dimples appeared in her cheeks. She was so wholesome. Miles returned with a bottle of Dr Pepper and handed it to Renee, thanking Jim as he took back the leash.

'That's Stan and Lisa,' Renee said to me, indicating the spotlit pair in the center of the room. 'They are so cute, he always says he loves her after their show is over.'

I surveyed the crowd clustered around Stan and Lisa. Among them, a very young, light-haired girl, about six months pregnant, had a collar and leash around her neck, but she was holding the handle of the leash herself. She had an intent look on her luminous face as she watched Stan, who was now flicking a cat-o'-nine-tails onto the expanse of Lisa's flesh, leaving little red stripes on her white skin. I couldn't take my eyes off the pregnant girl. What was she doing here? Why was she holding her own leash?

A stern 'Sit!' from Miles drew my attention away. To my surprise, Shelly and shackled Renee were now kissing! Miles let them make out for a few seconds, Renee half-standing to get a better purchase on Shelly, then he jerked back on her leash, forcing her to sit. Then it started up again.

'I don't think Trish would be too happy about you seeing this,' said Jim.

'Oh, this is where you draw the line?' I asked. 'Some chaperone.'

He smiled widely, and I could see he was missing a number of teeth on the side of his mouth. Miles checked his watch and stood up, leading Renee from her seat. She complimented me on my sundress, indenting her dimples with a smile. As they left, I saw that Kat had her boot on the prone, shackled man's sooty head and was resting it there, conquering, immobile, like a Victorian hunter posing for a daguerreotype with his foot on a dead lion. Shelly, alone now, watched from her chair. The dead-eyed look those women gave each other intrigued and frightened me. Jim took my arm. I glanced back at the pregnant girl, but she was gone; Stan and Lisa had vanished. When I looked to Kat again, her eyes were clamped on me with an impersonal, scrutinizing stare. I returned her gaze too long, I knew – too long to be right, too long for Aunt Trish.

That night, in the dark, awake under the covers on the lumpy couch in Kat's room, I lay in wait for memories of my Mr Brown: his long, pale fingers, the rough tweed of his worn jacket that smelled of pipe tobacco when I pressed my nose in it, the round toes of his brogans, the dull rose gold of his wedding band as it glinted in the half-light. He was so dear, so kind, my Mr Brown. He always caressed me with tender longing, as if saying goodbye. He taught my hands and my mouth with a solemn air, an educator even in his pleasure. Once, he drove me all the way to the shore during Easter break, our only foray outside the world of his little study. It was a warm, cloudy day in April. There were three people on the pebbly beach: a heavy man in khaki shorts and a wind-breaker; a small woman with frizzy, brown hair; and a tubby kid with a kite that wouldn't quite lift off the ground, though it kept making little, hopeful hops into the air.

Mr Brown and I pulled off our clothes. We both had on our bathing suits underneath. His was baggy green nylon. His legs were thin, the hair on them reddish. I was in my shiny blue swim team Speedo suit, the only one I owned. It made my chest look flat, which I resented. But Mr Brown knew better. We hobbled along for a while, the stones bruising our tender feet, until we came to a cluster of rocks, about fifty yards from where the people were. We sat and watched the gulls, creamy white, gliding against the ice-gray sky. He turned to me and said, 'You know that sand is just very finely ground rock.'

'Oh,' I said. 'That must take forever.'

'Millions of years,' he said, letting some sand sift through his long, curled fingers. I put my forefinger in the elastic band of his swim trunks and watched his eyes glaze over, as they always did when desire infused him. He was sitting with his back to the beach. No one could see. I firmly stroked those nylon swim trunks until he closed his eyes in rapture. Oh, heaven.

And when our days of tenderness were over, Mr Brown left me a virgin. Yes, after all that fuss, I lay on the couch in Aunt Trish's apartment as whole as the day I was born. I had tried to make it otherwise. I was desperate for Mr Brown to fuck me, but he said that was a step too far. I wanted to marry him. I had it all worked out: we would live in a little house in Massachusetts, or someplace else in the liberal far north; he would get a job at one of the fancy boarding schools up there, and I would spend the day getting myself ready for him, softening my skin, brushing my hair, plucking my eyebrows. Every night, my beloved would return to me, and come close to dying of pleasure. Mr Brown chuckled sadly when I recounted my fantasy, lowering his eyelids so I could see the veins through the papery skin, and said, 'Oh, my girl, no, you're made for better things.' That statement always made me feel lonely, because it implied an end to our affair but also because it hinted at some promise inside me that I was unaware of, like a tumor embedded in my flesh, making ready to bloom. I felt frightened of the future then, and huddled up against my lover's hard chest, seeking some hint of feminine softness, some extra bit of flesh to hang on to. But there was none. Mr Brown's body was stiff as a tree.

Still wakeful on the night of the whips and chains, I mulled over my life so far. I was a botch. I could see no future. I had no plans. I saw no example I wished to follow. I didn't want to be a nurse, or a stewardess, or a secretary; I didn't want to work in the meatpacking district or be a housewife. I just wanted to prowl around. I walked the streets endlessly. Watching people. I had a ravening mind; I wanted I wanted I wanted. I wanted into people's lives. I followed couples as they scurried down the street, carrying groceries and bunches of flowers, children tugging on their arms. I followed businessmen on their way from work. I followed elegantly dressed women who marched resolutely down the street and raised their hands for taxis. They were all bustling, all running, all rushing. Everyone in New York City seemed to have a purpose, except for me. I was driven by a need with no end, no goal. I was looking for love, I think, though that's not what it felt like at the time. At the time I felt hard and cold as a knife in the snow.

Knight

One time I followed this guy. His hair was a tangled web of blond curls that fell to hunched, narrow shoulders. He made me think of a cattail reed. It was wickedly cold, but all he was wearing was a pin-striped suit and a cashmere scarf. Sneakers. I walked out of work, saw him pass me by, and followed him all the way from Orchard Street to Twenty-third and First. He ducked into a coffee shop. I walked in behind him. He sat at the counter. I sat beside him. He ordered pea soup. I asked for hot chocolate. I looked at his face. He was older than I thought. At least twenty-five. His nose was red. He felt my stare, turned. His face was pale, with a high forehead and Nordic features, like a knight, it seemed to me. He looked right at me and shivered. 'Freezing,' he said, blowing into his cupped hands.

'You're not wearing enough,' I said.

'I thought I'd be straight in a cab,' he said. 'I always forget they change shifts this time of day.' His eyes passed over my body. 'You're all bundled up.'

'I always walk home from work,' I said.

His soup came, then my cocoa. We ignored each other for a few moments.

'What's your job?' he asked. 'If you don't mind –'

'I wait tables,' I said.

'That's a tough job.'

'Have you ever –?'

'No.'

I knew we would walk to his place. I wasn't thinking about making love; he was going to be my boyfriend, that was all. I was already imagining our apartment. It would have those round, paper globe shades on all the lights, and shelves filled with books. He was clearly a reader. So, after he finished his soup, said goodbye politely, and walked out, my cheeks burned with humiliation and loss.

Kitty

I knew Kat was no good for Aunt Trish, I saw she was playing her, but I was drawn to her in spite of myself. I guess I figured she was bad like me. Good people like Aunt Trish filled me with anxiety because I knew one day they would see I was just a destructive little fucker. Kat bought me clothes, tight jeans and floaty tops, platform shoes and huge hoop earrings. I was flattered by her attention. When Aunt Trish saw me in my new getups, she would click her tongue and blush, but she wouldn't say a word against Kat. All she'd say was 'You better not wear that when you go back home to visit.' That was her way of saying I better visit. My father called every few days to see how I was doing, and then Suky would get on the line. I missed her terribly, but when I heard that drug in her voice, I felt violence rising up in me. My voice went dead; I was abrupt, rude, horrible to her. Then I would hang up and cry, sob into my pillow, 'I was mean, I was mean,' and Trish would stroke my head until I fell asleep.

Kat always looked unrecognizable when she went to work in a cheap skirt suit and pumps, her thick hair teased to high heaven, lips slippery with gloss, eyelids iridescent blue. She looked like she was in drag. But one morning, after Trish left, as I washed the breakfast dishes, sponged down the table, swept the floor, Kat stood observing me in her dressing robe, her arms folded. I felt self-conscious and a little alarmed. Ever since the night at the club, when she had set her foot on that shackled man's head and stared at Shelly, I had known she was a little bit dangerous. That novel she was writing – I had read it, of course. It was full of sex. That's pretty much all it was. It was

113

a book about a young woman named Kitty, and her adventures with other women. Kitty went prowling around hunting for pleasure. When she saw a girl she liked, she pounced. It didn't matter if her prey was a married woman of fifty or a child of twelve. Kitty always got her girl. I read the latest installment every night when I went to bed. It made such an impression on me that I committed one passage of her prose to heart:

> *Kitty looked at Mrs Washington. Though no longer young, she had smoky black eyes and a long neck, her breasts were full, her hair lustrous. There was no way Kitty was going to spend one more night as a guest in this woman's country estate without slipping a finger in her pussy.*

Kat made sense to me once I started reading her novel. I had seen part of a porn film once; two of my brothers, the Dim Twins, took me into New Haven to buy Christmas presents for the rest of the family. We each had our savings in our pockets – in our godly family, you were expected to save your allowance all year to buy presents for your siblings. Once we stepped off the train, Rob and Griffin, both thirteen, took me by the hand and said we were watching a movie and *then* buying the presents. I was eight. We got into the theater only because we were short enough to creep by the booth without the ticket collector seeing us. My brothers had bought me a lollipop to keep me occupied, and I, in my innocence, sat licking the thing as the opening credits came up.

In the first scene, a woman was lying on a couch in a silk nightie. There was a knock on the door. She opened it. It was the TV repairman. Within twenty seconds, the two of them were in a clump on the couch, jerking around. Griffin, the brother to my right, had his hand in his pants at this point, and I whacked him on the side of the head. The tussle that ensued, with the three of us clamped onto one another, arms flailing like some crazy octopus, me scratching and biting the twins and they spitting into my face and head-butting me, attracted an usher, who led us out fast, cursing. I came away from that incident with a bloody nose, and the certainty that you had to get to the point fast in dirty movies. And Kat sure did that. Her alter ego, Kitty, didn't waste a second. No sooner did she arrive at the ornate country mansion than she was feeling up the parlor maid and pressing up against her hostess.

At first, I thought I was reading the manuscript behind Kat's back. But I think she must have noticed that it changed location, because after that first time, she made sure she left it in a neat pile right by my bed. Every morning during breakfast, she would look at me and wink. Poor Aunt Trish. I don't know how much she knew about Kat. Yet how could she not have known? There was Kat's obscene friend Shelly, the 'actress,' who, despite being 'based in San Francisco,' was in and out of the apartment every few weeks; there was the hypersexy, slightly spastic way Kat moved and spoke – not to mention what she was writing . . . Well, I guess the thing was, Trish loved Kat, and she wanted to believe she was loved in return.

That morning, as I knelt under the table, sweeping up the crumbs from under her seat, Kat contemplated me silently for a long time. And then finally she said, 'What do you want to be when you grow up?' I sat back on my haunches, looked up at her, and shrugged.

'Well,' she said, 'what are you good at?' The thought of Mr Brown closing his eyes at the beach, astonishment on his face as I touched him slowly and deliberately, came into my mind.

'Nothing,' I said.

'You have to have some kind of talent.'

I shrugged. 'Not everybody has talent.'

'People who don't have talent are usually nice,' said Kat. 'Are you nice?'

I saw Suky, slumped on the side of Trish's couch as though she had been shot. I shook my head.

'Well then, you'd better have talent,' said Kat.

'What are you on my case for?' I asked.

'I believe in you, kid,' she said. And then she went into the bathroom to turn herself into someone's secretary. When she came back, she pretended to have an idea on the spot. She needed some dirty pictures to illustrate her novel. She wanted me to be her Kitty. I thought about it for a few seconds. 'I'll pay you, too, if the book gets published.'

'Okay,' I said.

Getting naked was the easy part. It was the outfits I balked at. Kat had been hoarding them in the closet of her office in a big, cardboard box marked 'Kitchen Supplies.' There were riding breeches with the crotch cut out, a stewardess dress with snap-on boob covers, a rubber cat suit. It was absurd. I couldn't stop laughing. Especially since Suky had basically been doing this to me since infancy: I was dressed up as Mae West at three, Jayne Mansfield at seven. Suky kept all my dress-up duds in a wooden box we called the 'fun box.' Even now that Suky has left me – having politely, obligingly, and without fuss stopped breathing one foggy evening – even now I believe those bizarre and slightly creepy albums are stored somewhere in Chester's basement. The pages may be disintegrating, eaten out by the acid in the cheap paper, but if you were to open one of those leatherette volumes, you would be surprised to find not pictures of four boys and a girl, a healthy, happy family of the local pastor, but the likeness of only one child, a blonde, sloe-eyed girl in a skimpy dress and feather boa, staring the camera down. Pippa at one, at two, at three and five, at seven to fourteen, her expressions moving, as the years went by, from innocent cheer to a knowing, sullen stare, and finally to full-fledged hatred. So, I was a natural. Kat couldn't believe it. I had no shyness at all in front of the camera. I looked at it as if it were a person I knew and didn't like. That's what she said, anyway. She said it was 'pure Kitty.' Kitty, she explained, was every woman's wild side. She was fearless.

'Don't you wish *you* were fearless?' she asked as she reloaded her battered Canon.

'I guess so,' I said.

'You act hard, but you're a marshmallow. If you were fearless you wouldn't cry every time you hang up the phone after talking to your mother. You would forget the past. You would look ahead.'

'Is that what you do?'

'Oh, baby. I'm the girl from Pluto. I'm the scary thing.'

'How did you ever get hooked up with Aunt Trish?'

'I know, right? But she loves me. She's my Momma. Not everything has to make sense, Chicklet.'

The next morning she came bouncing out of the bathroom in her sweats, shadowboxing. No work today; she'd called in sick. The doorbell rang. Shelly burst in, her naturally amplified voice bouncing around her spacious rib cage. She let out a Texan 'Whoop!' then started pawing through Aunt Trish's record collection, derisively holding up a Carole King album.

'Don't even bother,' said Kat, producing a cardboard box from under the electric piano. 'Check mine out.' They put on 'Knock on Wood' and danced to Otis Redding singing 'I better knock – on wood, yeah . . .' Shelly's dance was obscene, her thick pelvis thrusting forward again and again, an ugly frown on her face, her arms in the air, big, hard breasts stretching her sweater. 'Let's get this show on the road!' she bellowed. Kat oozed to the downbeat, her eyes hooded, glazed, private. She touched my wrist very lightly, drawing me in. I began to move to the music, aware, somehow, of turning my back on good Aunt Trish and entering a poisonous, glimmering circle. I felt a sharp, defiant joy at my recklessness.

Shelly had been cast in the part of Mrs Washington, the wealthy woman whom Kitty seduces in her country mansion. So this session was going to involve a certain amount of *reenactment*. In a trance of creativity, wearing a new, self-important face, Kat placed the lights, chose the costumes, set the scene: I am dressed in a pair of large white girls' underwear, a pointy black bra, and high-heeled, black fetish shoes. I am stealing Mrs Washington's pearls. Mrs Washington walks in, dressed in her riding clothes. She looks imperious. Infuriated by my crime, she decides I am in need of a beating. This was a still photo we were posing for, yet Kat directed us as though it were a scene in a film. Shelly got herself so worked up when she discovered me that she actually wept with rage. Kat was over the moon about her performance.

But now, having so utterly nailed this preamble, our director was confounded by a technical dilemma: when Mrs Washington gave me my lashes, how were we to make the scene seem real without hurting me? Kat suggested that Shelly grab the rubber paddle conveniently stowed on the mantelpiece and bring it down to just above the skin of my buttocks, so it looked like she was spanking me. Shelly tried, but her aim was off, you might say. She brought the thing down so hard I let out a yelp. A little red welt rose up on my butt; I craned my neck to see it. At first, Kat rushed toward me, to see if I was hurt. But something in my astonished expression must have told her I was feeling all right. 'Shall we try that again?' she asked quietly. I nodded.

So we took a little detour from illustrating Kat's book. At first, I couldn't believe it was happening. I mean, don't get me wrong; if I cut my finger, I say 'ow,' like everyone else. But there was something about the circumstances here, the setup, the elaborate way I was tied to the table or the bed or the radiator. The pain was different from stubbing my toe. If it went on long enough, if I was spanked or whipped or slapped long enough, my skin went cold and tingling, I was able to bust through the pain, leaving the reality of the moment, into another place where I couldn't really see anything in focus. The feeling I had there was serene, silent, empty, euphoric. My Feeling reminds me of the happiest born-agains, ones I've seen on TV, when their eyes roll back in their heads and they raise their arms, out of their minds on bliss. This particular ecstasy was limited to those few weeks with Kat and Shelly. I have never been able to pass through pain that way again. Or haven't allowed myself to.

Fever

Here's the thing we didn't think of: one afternoon, Aunt Trish came home from work with a fever. She turned the key in the lock, heard Gladys Knight blasting out of her bedroom, hurried in, and found me manacled to the bed with the skirt of a pink crinoline gown over my head, being slapped by Shelly as Kat photographed us, shouting, 'Great! Do that again. Freeze. Okay! Beautiful!' Aunt Trish was standing there, pale, shivering, and horrified, when I turned and saw her.

I moved out that afternoon, while Aunt Trish was sleeping off her flu, having called the police and watched the woman she loved flee her apartment. I couldn't bear to be there when she woke up; I was too ashamed.

The only person I knew in New York, aside from Aunt Trish, was Jim, the diabetic with the missing toe. His apartment was in a Brooklyn basement with a sizable garden. He stayed there rent free, because his old friend Roy, a drug dealer in his fifties, kept some of his supply stashed in Jim's broom closet and various other locations in the apartment. Jim also sold drugs for Roy on occasion. Kat had taken me to his place a few times. Jim always doled out shortbread cookies and black coffee, then handed Kat a brown paper bag as she was leaving. This sideline, along with disability checks for his diabetes, enabled Jim to live the life of an artist and man-about-town. Though well below the poverty line, he always had a bit of cash on hand, and he welcomed me to his modest home like a visiting queen.

I had the sense, as I dropped my duffel bag on Jim's shiny floor painted the color of pomegranates, that I was slipping off the edge of what I had known the world to be and floating in dangerous space. Aunt Trish had been family. Jim was unknown territory, a new life. Suky would go crazy if she knew. My excitement was liberally spiked with guilt. I would call her soon. I would. But for now, I sat at Jim's kitchen table, sipping strong coffee brewed on a paint-spattered double burner and eating a piece of buttery shortbread. The hot coffee melted the sweet, rich cookie in my mouth. I looked out the glass of his back door, into his tiny garden, walled off by a fence of old painted doors.

Everything in the little apartment had been considered in some way, was either lovely or bizarre or instructive. The shelves were packed with books about everything from cave painting to rocket design: *Nuns' Habits Through the Ages. The Art of Holograms Revealed.* I spent hours that first afternoon flipping through books, learning about painters, mostly, from Piero della Francesca to Bonnard, Manet to Pollock. Jim's work was stacked neatly, facing the wall. Shyly, he turned a piece around to show me. It was a collage made up of countless shreds of paper, movie tickets, newspaper clippings, warning labels, which all cohered to make a landscape. It was obsessively constructed, but the composition reminded me of the paint-by-numbers sets I used to work on when I was a kid. Until I found the little figures hidden in the rocks or the shrubbery – incongruous beer maids peeled off of beer bottles, the man on the Mr Clean bottle, a naked calendar girl. Jim would Xerox the images and shrink them, so they looked like evil elves lurking in a pleasant countryside constructed out of refuse.

Jim rarely sold his work, he had no gallery, but he was ferociously dedicated. He would wake late – eleven or twelve – then perform his elaborate toilette, which included applying a light coat of Elizabeth Arden foundation makeup to his sallow skin and covering his thinning pate with black shoe polish. Only then did he begin to work, sorting through the bins of scrap paper, bits of rag, string, hair – anything to make his landscapes thrum with color and texture. In lieu of rent, I was sent out some mornings to look for material, and I would root around in the garbage, on the street, in magazine racks, for the perfect scarlet, the most acid cerulean.

At three in the afternoon, I went to work. I had found another restaurant, down the street, to hone my serving skills in. When I got off, at nine, Jim was just hitting his stride. I marveled at his ability to work all day, stop to make some inventive pasta dish for the two of us, then go back to his labors for another six or seven hours, finally smoking a joint and hitting the sack at dawn. He would do this for days at a time, then take a few days off and sleep. He was surprised the first night I came home from work bone tired, stood by him as he fitted a torn corner of salmon pink tissue paper onto the rectangle of board on the table, and said, 'Can I have some?'

'Have some what?' he asked.

'Speed.' He looked up at me, surprised but smiling. 'How do you know?'

'That's the one I know about,' I said.

'How old are you now?' he asked, crinkling his forehead.

'Seventeen.'

'Did you graduate from high school yet?'

'That's what I want it for. The test is next Thursday. I have to study.'

'You can have a little,' he said. 'But don't overdo it. By Thursday you'll be insane.' So he gave me a round, white pill that he kept in a misshapen ceramic pinch pot on a shelf next to the sea salt. I swallowed it. The speed hit me hard, like the smell of ammonia. Everything in the room snapped into extreme focus; it all seemed extra clean, and bright. I hadn't felt so awake, so cheerful, so filled with purpose since the day I swallowed ten of Suky's finest back in junior high. 'One thing you can't do,' Jim said, 'is start talking. You start talking on this stuff, you never stop.' I retreated to my makeshift bedroom – a daybed blocked from the rest of the room by a swath of old pink silk – and read two entire books, one on history, one on math. Hitherto ungraspable concepts glided into my mind like melted butter into pancake batter.

I emerged from my lair to tell Jim how incredibly smart I had become, he said something in response, and we were off. We talked for six hours straight, said things so perceptive and profound that it amazed us no one in the history of the world had yet come up with them. Jim even took notes, our ideas were so brilliant. Finally, we crashed. When we woke, hours later, to read the scrawled notes he had written during our jam session, and found that they contained pearls of wisdom such as 'flounder are bottom-feeders, hence should never be eaten with carrots or other vegetables which grow underground or you are liable to develop depressions, NUTRITION IS EVERYTHING,' I was dumbfounded, but Jim just nodded his head with a rueful smile. When I opened the history and math books that I had wolfed down, I recognized next to nothing, except what I had already gone over the old-fashioned, nondrug-induced way, so I went back to my old method of studying. I passed the high school equivalency test.

Surprisingly, Jim had a girlfriend: a Swedish woman named Olla. She was around forty, an artist, very kind to Jim, and she didn't seem to mind me hanging around. We would go out sometimes, the three of us, to museums or movies. Jim and Olla taught me about painting, the history of it and the point of it. I came to recognize different periods, different artists. I went to the galleries and even started forming my own opinions about the new art.

Jim had reminded me how harmless he was so many times that I figured sex was not a part of his life anymore. He would lounge around the apartment with his socks off, feet up. The smooth gap left by his missing pinkie toe made him seem curiously unreal, like an imperfect doll. But Olla was always kissing him, making much of him, and guiding him gently into his bedroom for an hour or so at a time while I sat in the garden, or did the dishes, or went out on a walk. I liked Olla, and I was determined to seem as nonthreatening as possible. After Mr Brown and Aunt Trish, I didn't want to wreck anyone's life, and I didn't want to end up on the street, either.

Crash

I still don't know the reason for what happened next. I don't understand it. I mean, I was doing relatively well. I had a job, a place to live, friends, I had finished school.

It started with a normal dose of speed one night. We were all going out dancing: me, Jim, Olla, and a bunch of their friends, hard-core bohemians in their forties, missing the occasional tooth. I hardly ever went out anywhere, so it was a big night for me; I didn't want to drag around exhausted from work. I danced all night, and in the morning I just couldn't bear the idea of going to bed and waking up with my head raw and jangled, my thoughts morose. So I swallowed some more, to keep up the happiness. Jim didn't know. He wasn't counting his stash. I went to work high and slapped those plates of eggs Florentine and Belgian waffles onto the tables so quick that whipped cream and hollandaise sauce spattered all over my arms. A few customers needed sponging down, but at least they got fast service.

That night, I decided to go out on my own and see what happened. Before I left, I got up on my tiptoes and reached into the clumsy clay speed pot like a kid filching M&M's. By now I had been levitating for forty-eight hours. I was starting to feel omnipotent. I took the 2 Train into Manhattan with no idea of where I was going, jumped out of my seat at Fourteenth Street. Hot air laced with feces swirled around the platform as I hurried out of the train. There was a sound in my head, a high, metallic whistle. My movements were fluid, precise, like those of a perfect machine. My mind felt spotless, sterilized, my thoughts gleamed like stainless steel. The people and cars around me, by contrast, were pulsing in a staggered, irregular pattern, freezing one moment,

127

then oozing by in slow motion the next, as though time had become as elastic as toffee. A gleaming scenario played and replayed itself in my head with razorlike precision; I was going to find that pregnant girl with the flaxen hair who was holding on to her own leash, the one I had seen the time I came to the club with Kat and Shelly, and I was going to save her life. I would track her down in her filthy squat and swoop in like a commando, excise her from her perverted existence, buy her a square meal, take her home to Olla and Jim. We would all live together, the five of us, a family. Her child would be fair, with violet eyes and a saintly disposition.

I searched the streets around there, trying to find the club Shelly had taken us to. All I could remember was five steps down, a metal door. At last, I found it. The sweaty, sharp-eyed woman behind the Plexiglas booth looked up from her book. She didn't know anything about the pregnant girl. She told me this was her first night of work here, and she couldn't stand the fucking heat.

I pushed the heavy plastic fringe aside, ducking my head, and emerged into the windowless library. The ceiling was very low. There was no music on. Purple and red lights flashed mutely. As I walked in, the few souls wandering around the room eyed me hungrily, like bored guests at a failing party, sizing up a new arrival. I wondered whether I was moving strangely. Music came on – a rigid beat. I walked into the back room, a kind of cave, also lined with paperbacks, and pierced with tiny cubicles. On a narrow stage, a middle-aged woman in a leather corset danced for a middle-aged man. The door of one of the cubicles swung open; a male figure emerged and walked away fast, head down. A light-haired, slender girl remained in the cubicle, her back to me, buttoning her blouse. I stood, waiting. She swiveled around and looked at me expectantly. She was young, but her face was puffy and slack. 'I thought you might be someone else,' I said, turning.

Back in the main room, Lisa and Stan were setting up their act. Maybe the pregnant girl would be coming in later. She had loved Stan and Lisa. Remember how she had stood, transfixed, her wide eyes unblinking, her small hand grasping the handle of her leash, as though her owner had abandoned her? A spotlight came on, illuminating the pair. I walked up to them and stood just inside that pool of light, exactly where I had seen the pregnant girl standing. I was almost close enough to touch them. Others gathered around them, too, waiting for the performance to begin, eyes glazed, hungry and vacant.

Lisa lay on the low bed. She was blindfolded with a band of black leather. Her bare belly was pale and flaccid, a concave hammock of flesh hung between two wide-set, mountainous hip bones. Her large breasts spread out across her chest. The skin around the nipples was crowded with marks. Some of them looked like cat scratches. Others were raised, like burns, or white, old scars. Stan tipped a metal beaker of molten wax, letting a fine thread of it dribble onto her skin, precise as an alchemist. As the wax hit her skin, Lisa flinched and turned her head to the side. I gawked with the others as the pool of wax turned white and hard. Later, when Stan knelt to untie her blindfold, Lisa looked up at him adoringly with unfocused sapphire eyes and mouthed, 'I love you.' I felt embarrassed to witness this sudden moment of intimacy. The other observers had melted away. I stood fast, unable to budge, flashing lights throbbing in my peripheral vision. Lisa sat up as if alone, heels together, legs flopping open, and started peeling dried wax off her tits. Stan looked up me curiously, then bent to unplug his hot plate.

A man approached me then. He was narrow hipped, effeminate, with full lips and a halo of dark curls. The first three buttons of his tight, silky shirt were open and revealed a tawny, hairless chest.

'Hey, you all right?' he asked. I told him I was looking for someone. He had never seen the pregnant girl. I smiled and talked to him, feeling so charming as I moved really fast and jerked my arms around. All I can remember of our conversation is the effeminate man saying most people thought he was gay, but he was straight – *with a twist*. He said that several times. His name was Mandy. I don't remember how it happened that I asked him to drive me to Connecticut, but there we were, at dawn, on Route 84 heading toward Danbury in his tangerine Camaro. Mandy told me about his life – how he was in auto sales with his father, how he had appeared in seven of his father's commercials, starting from the age of three. I was barely listening. I was scared to see Suky.

We stopped for a pee at a truck stop on the outskirts of Danbury. He took a little Chinese purse embroidered with a dragon out of his glove compartment, unzipped it, and held it open so I could see: white powder in a plastic bag. Feeling myself coming down slightly, I snorted a staggered white zigzag of powder off a glossy car sales brochure. As I sniffed the line through a dollar bill, felt the acidic, chemical kick in the back of my throat, I read: '200 dollars cash back with every new Nissan truck purchased!'

There was a picture of a stocky man on the brochure. He was standing beside a red truck. He had a mustache, and Mandy's full lips. Mandy's dad, no doubt, smiling up at me. I felt a little sorry for the guy, given what I was using his face for. I knew the cocaine was a mistake as I snorted it. Combined with all the amphetamines I had taken in the last two days, it clamped down on my mind like a set of iron teeth. Every noise sounded like danger to me. My chauffeur's profile, with its aquiline nose and plump mouth, seemed malign. I imagined him cutting me into lamb-chop-size chunks and tossing them gaily out the window all the way to Suky's house. At every stoplight I imagined opening the door and escaping.

We drove up to the Delton Green at twenty to seven. 'I've done a lot of crazy things,' said Mandy. 'But this takes the cake. You said your father is a minister?' I nodded. 'Yup. This takes the fuckin' cake.' He made ready to get out. 'Oh,' I said. 'Do you mind waiting for a little, um, and then I'll ... come get you ... if ...' He turned up the radio and sank down in the seat, nodding with a louche expression. Wondering what I had promised him, I walked to the side door of the house. The first birds were singing. The air smelled sweet and clean. I picked up the hollow plastic rock beside the welcome mat, ripped the silver key off its Velcro square, turned it in the lock.

The house was quiet and warm. I walked into the kitchen. The clock was ticking. It sounded so loud. The house smelled yeasty, sugary, as it always had. I was suddenly very hungry. I looked in the bread bin. There were three cinnamon donuts in there. I took one and bit into it, crunched the sandy sugar between my teeth. It felt so good to be home. Such a relief. I heard a sound on the stairs. I turned. The decline in her appearance was shocking. Her pale skin was luminous, almost translucent, the skin around her eyes dark, her red hair lank and stringy. She had lost weight. She started to scream, then she put her hand to her mouth and wept.

'Thank God,' she said.

'I'm a high school graduate, Mommy,' I said. My voice sounded completely foreign to me. I must have been talking very loud. 'Ssh,' she said. 'Your father.' I whispered now, expanding on how well I had done on the test, exaggerating my results, believing myself instantly. She hugged me. I just let her, at first, my arms dangling at my sides. After a while, though, I put my arms around her and pressed her to me. She felt so fragile, like a bird.

We embraced for a long time. Then I made her put her feet on my feet. She was sort of giggling, embarrassed, but I insisted she do it, just the way I had put my feet over hers when I was little. And we danced. Her face was so close to mine. I could see the new wrinkles around her eyes. The flesh over her eye sockets was sinking. Her breath was minty. She was looking up at me with deep affection – our old intimacy, as if we were the only two people in the world, as if we were newlyweds. I glanced at the clock. A few seconds to seven. Almost time for her first dose. She never missed it. The minute hand thumped into place beneath the twelve. Seven o'clock. She gently began to release her hold on me. A spike of anger went through me then. I held my arms rigid. She put her hand on my forearm, pushing me away a little. 'Okay, honey,' she said.

'You have an appointment?' I asked. She must have seen murder in my face, because she looked frightened.

'Let me go,' she said in her squeaky drawl.

Then I put my face close to hers. 'Look in my eyes,' I said. 'You see anything?' She was struggling to get out of my grip now; I had her by the shoulders, I was moving her to the wall, I didn't know what I was going to do to her, but I hated her so much, I wanted to kill her. 'I'm like you now, Suky, see? I'm fucking high like you wish you were right now, you little junkie!'

Her face twisted into a grimace of rage and indignation. She bared her teeth, spit formed on the edges of her mouth, her eyes narrowed, she called me a liar, a runaway, an addict. She actually looked like she was turning into an animal. It was terrifying. She wanted her dose. I had her pinned to the wall. She was hissing, 'Get out get out get out get out!' Her bones felt so flimsy I could have snapped them. I took a fistful of her hair, held her head back. Her eyes widened, scared, expectant. I had no idea what to do next. So I kissed her, on the mouth. Passed my hand over her nipples. I felt like I was slashing her throat with a knife. Looking back on it, it seems overdramatic, but at seventeen, a blizzard of coke and speed racing through my head, I thought I was saying it all: I was telling my mother that she had treated me like a lover and a baby, a possession, but not a person, never a person. I think she got the message. Anyway, she started screaming. She was just screaming and screaming, and Des thundered downstairs in his brown robe, growling like a grizzly. That was my signal. I ran straight into Mandy's Camaro, tears streaming down my face, wiping my mouth like there was shit on it.

By the time we got back to New York, I was curled up in a ball, staring out the window. Understandably, Mandy was sick of me. He dropped me at the entrance to the Lincoln Tunnel, saying,

'You're a downer, man,' and he was off to Jersey, where the girls are sunny. I walked to the subway and got back to Jim's apartment just as he and Olla were getting up. They were relieved to see me. They asked no questions. We all had coffee and shortbread cookies, and Olla tenderly laid out one of her pretty sundresses for me to wear when I woke. She put it out on a chair, where I could see it, to cheer me up. I lay my head on her lap as she stroked my forehead. I could feel the soft pillow of her bosom on my ear. I slept and slept, and when I opened my eyes, it seems to me now, it was three years later, I was twenty and living on Orchard Street.

A Brief Catalog of Sins

I remember the years after I kissed Suky in fragmented clusters, as though seen on a TV with rotten reception. I can flip through the channels as often as I like, but no narrative coheres. All I can glimpse is fixes I got myself into. Not how, not why. I see a young Finnish actor lying beside me, so thin, like a boy, except for his phallus, which stands wavering nobly. I see his girlfriend, Oxanna, sitting beside me in a restaurant as the boy hands us each a bunch of roses. I see myself on the street being slapped by a woman with short black hair and a livid face. I see myself lying on a table. A man wearing a wedding ring is standing between my open legs (somewhere in here I must have lost my virginity). And, like snowy static, I see pills – pink pills, white pills, blue pills – falling across the screen. Okay, I understand, of course, I took every pill I could get my hands on, no wonder I can't remember anything. Wait, I can see an ashtray littered with cigarette butts on a coffee table. A man – Sergei – clamps a cigarette between his thick, sensual lips, lights up, and inhales deeply, with real enjoyment, his bulging, black eyes open wide. I see the man's wife, Amelia, also Russian. She is blonde, very thin, exhausted looking. I work for these people. I teach their daughter English. Her name is Anya. Sergei is glowering, emphatic. The skin on his arms is very smooth, tawny, and hairless. His body is of an almost comical shape – potbelly, short, muscular legs. He is a Trotskyite and a cellist. He plays for me. Dense, dark waves of music rise from beneath his fingers. I find the sound powerful, melancholy, hypnotic. Sometimes I spend the night here so I don't have to go all the way downtown on the subway. On these occasions, Sergei reads out loud to me from

'The Revolution Betrayed'. I see myself kneeling in front of the couch, Sergei's penis in my mouth, while his wife and daughter sleep next door. How much worse can this get?

At around this time, the images become so flimsy, I can't make them out. I see my hands bound together at the back. I strain to catch a glimpse of myself, I worry, what the hell am I doing now? Then a clear color image quickens: I see people holding plastic cups filled with wine, talking. I see myself in lace-up leather boots, white-blonde hair, a muddy coat. My skin is pale, there are circles under my eyes. I am here with friends, ah yes, now it is all coming clear, I see better now, wait, now I'm inside the screen, I am standing next to myself, I can't believe how real this all is, I can hear the voices – it's an art opening. These are the people I used to serve margaritas to at El Corazón! Remember? The ones with paint on their hands. What are they doing here? My boyfriend, Craig, the skinny one with the poker face, is standing beside his painting, a hyperrealistic rendering of a sink filled with dirty dishes. There is a red dot beside it. Our friends cluster around us. Jed, a very tall, part-Sioux sculptor from Nebraska City, his heavy work boots spread wide, checked woolen jacket flapping open, congratulates Craig. 'You are one lucky fuck, man, Gigi Lee is a major collector.' Jed looks over at a very beautiful woman in her forties with a nearly impossibly large bust and tiny waist, wearing a cat suit, her long black hair falling to her waist. Her lovely face is surprisingly tired looking, and her voluptuous mouth droops at the corners, as though it has been borrowed from someone else. Jed the Sioux now puts his hand on the small of my back. Have I got it wrong? Is Jed my boyfriend? Terry, the short young woman from El Corazón, with a soft, exposed midriff, chunky high heels, and a cartoonish, glossy red mouth, says, 'She's an heiress.' Now the beauty in the cat suit walks over to the ratty little clump of us and looks up at Craig with an impish smile.

'I love my painting.' She has a thick Italian accent.

Craig clears his throat. 'I'm ... glad you bought it.'

'I am Gigi Lee.'

'I know. Nice to meet you.' Craig shakes her hand stiffly.

'You like to paint from the sea?' she asks.

'I usually paint in the studio,' says Craig. 'From photographs.'

'You must come to our house at the sea, you could make a beautiful painting of it,' says Gigi. Then, turning to acknowledge the rest of us, 'You must all come this weekend. Stay the night!' Craig introduces each of us. Gigi nods at us all, her tiny nose pulling itself in like a turtle seeking its shell. 'Herb!' she calls. An older man walks out of the crowd. He must be in his fifties. Swarthy, with deep creases in his skin, a crooked nose, and clear blue eyes, he has an open, amused expression on his face. 'I want them all to come to the party,' Gigi says, opening her arms.

'The more the merrier,' says Herb drily, teasing.

'It is this weekend. You can come? There is a bus if you have no car.'

'I have a car,' says Craig. I nod. Craig has hit a vein of gold, a big commission. And the prospect of free food and drink is something none of us will pass up.

*

We are all in Craig's car, a vast vanilla 1967 Riviera convertible with crimson upholstery. The car used to belong to Craig's deceased aunt Ginny. I am beginning to remember that Terry, the girl with the smirking red mouth, and I sleep with either poker-faced Craig, Jed the elegant Sioux sculptor, or ornery Calvin, the chunky abstract painter. Don't get me wrong; this is not a free love situation. It's a rotation. Each of us is the girlfriend of one or another of these three guys at any given time. Occasionally, a third girl is brought into the group from outside, but usually it's just Terry and I, so one of the guys is single for a while and becomes neutered, essentially another female, hanging out with us girls and whining about his loveless status, until a pregnant lull in the conversation when one of us is alone with him. Eyes lock, and away we go; he's a man again. Now it's someone else's turn to be single. We have managed this game of musical genitalia for over a year without much jealousy, our friendships intact. But all that is about to change, for me anyway. As I lean my head back on Aunt Ginny's red leather seat, the wind in my mouth, I have no idea that I am driving straight out of one life and into another.

Their house was right by the sea; Gigi had told us that much in her vague directions. We drove slowly beside the long hedge that hid the big houses, looking for their name. At last we found it: 'Lee,' painted in light blue script on a white mailbox. We turned in to the gravel driveway and drove toward the strangest building I had ever seen. It was a huge glass box with one metal wall. Inside the box was a small, old-fashioned yellow cottage with a red door – a house in a house. It was the middle of the afternoon; there were several cars parked in the driveway. As we approached the Lee home, we could see white leather couches in the outer, modern part of the dwelling. We knocked on the tall metal door of the outer shell. A doleful looking, middle-aged man answered. His shirt was half-untucked. He ushered us in with some sort of Eastern European accent, asked us mournfully if we would like some iced tea. We said yes. He took it like bad news and disappeared. A small, dark, smiling woman in a light green uniform bustled in carrying a tray of glasses filled with amber liquid. The Eastern European man picked up a couple of our bags and made for the stairs.

'That's okay,' said Craig.

'We'll get 'em,' said Calvin. The man stayed them with a raised hand. 'Please,' he said. He had a way about him that made it hard to tell if he was kidding, as though someone had dared him to pretend to be the butler for the afternoon. 'Mr and Mrs Lee are on the beach with the other guests,' he said, gesturing to a set of French doors that looked onto the sea. 'Mrs Lee says, come down if you like, or relax up here. Whatever you prefer.'

'Thanks,' said ornery Calvin, grabbing a handful of salted

peanuts from a large clamshell on the coffee table and looking up at a ten-foot abstract painting on the landing. 'Fucking Dieter Carlson,' he snarled through a mouthful of nuts. 'He's everywhere. And he can't even paint.'

Poker-faced Craig had ventured out onto the porch. I followed and stood beside him. I felt I was standing on the prow of a huge, beached ship. The sky stretched up from the horizon, a dome over our heads; occasional perfectly formed clouds were frozen in the blue expanse. All below – glittering water, white-blond sand – was awash in heat and light.

'Can you imagine owning a house like this?' I asked.

'We do own it, honey,' said Craig, his hand sliding down my back. 'I just bought it, remember?' I leaned on the railing and surveyed the beach. Several people were having a picnic down there. A woman in a red bathing suit and long black hair – Gigi – was wading in the water. Several others reclined on multi-colored bath towels. I sipped the sweet, cold tea. The best I'd had in my life. 'We probably shouldn't have invited so many people with a new cook in the kitchen,' I said.

'They'll be so drunk, they won't notice the food,' said Craig with a convincing drawl. He took to the role of a rich man easily. In fact, he was poised for a huge success; within ten years he would be one of the highest priced artists of his generation.

The others ambled onto the porch. 'I'm gonna go down to the beach,' said Jed, our current odd man out. 'Maybe there's a single lady down there in need of a real man.' Terry and Calvin smoked in silence. Gigi was looking up at us now and waving. We all descended the splintered wooden stairs to a narrow path that led us down the dune. I clung to the fantasy of ownership, breathing in the salty air, looking back at the gleaming glass house proprietarily. 'We have to get those stairs fixed,' said Craig in his deadened voice. When we got to the beach, though, it was over.

Gigi was on her belly, recumbent on a cerulean towel, a cherry red bathing suit clinging to her impossible form. Her black hair was drying in brittle, serpentine waves down her back. As we approached, she propped herself up on her elbows, clamping together her cleavage. 'Hello!' she said. A bronzed, lithe young man sat beside her. He had a sharp-ridged, hawklike nose, which seemed to stretch the skin on his face very taut. He gave us a surprised look from under bushy black brows. We must have looked like aliens, the druggy-pale, black-clad, sleep-deprived clutch of us standing on that costly stretch of coastline.

'This is Sam Shapiro, the novelist,' Gigi announced. 'Sam, this is Craig Simms, the painter I was telling you about. And these are his friends, let me see . . .' Craig introduced us all again. Gigi smiled at us vaguely, taking nothing in. I was hot in my dress, socks, and boots. 'Do you have your bathing suits?' Gigi asked. I had mine on under my dress, but I didn't feel ready to reveal my pasty form to this goddess. Gigi jumped up and took Craig by the arm. 'Come,' she said. 'Let's discuss the commission.' They were off. Jed sat on the sand, legs splayed, his ancient black raincoat spread out behind him, ebony hair glistening down his back, and glared at the sea.

'It's fucking hot,' said Terry, tugging off her T-shirt. Her bright purple bra encased large, soft breasts that jiggled like mounds of custard.

Sam smiled. 'Don't mind me,' he said.

'I don't,' said Terry, leaning back on her elbows and squinting at him.

Ornery Calvin lit a cigarette. 'So there's going to be a party tonight?' he said.

'There's always a party at Gigi's house,' said Sam.

I got up and walked toward the water. When no one seemed to be watching me, I unzipped my tattered thrift store dress, unlaced my boots, rolled my sweaty socks off my feet, and left it all in a neat pile. My bikini top didn't match the bottom. I was hoping people would think this was intentional. My icy blonde hair, fried by Terry's dubious skills as a colorist, was wound up into two little onions at the top of my head. I walked into the water, looking down at my skinny, pallid body. The water felt cold. I splashed the backs of my knees, then dove under a wave and swam a few strokes. When I came up, I was less than a yard away from two men paddling in the water, talking. I recognized one of them as Herb Lee, Gigi's husband. He had a cigar in his mouth. The other man was wearing thick, black-framed glasses. His hair was wild and graying. 'I don't see how you can possibly think,' he was saying, 'that I should cram all that into part one.'

'It's like I told you,' said Herb in his deep New York yet somehow aristocratic voice. 'Those scenes *belong* to the childhood.'

'But I'm moving back and forth in time. That's the structure of the thing! The narrative is *liquid*.'

'What I'm saying is,' answered Herb, 'let the sequences build up more power – less staccato. You want it to be a good read, don't you?' I had drifted a little closer to them by now and was eavesdropping shamelessly. Herb turned and acknowledged me. 'Hello,' he said. 'Are you with our party?'

'I'm with Craig, you bought his painting? We met at the opening . . .'

'Oh yes, sorry, this is Max Kessler, Max this is . . .'

'Pippa Sarkissian.'

'What kind of a name is that?'

'Swedish and Armenian.' Max Kessler had paddled away and was struggling toward the shore, dragging his feet through the undercurrent, his black swim trunks clinging to his legs, shoulders bowed.

'You're very welcome, Pippa,' said Herb, the laugh lines driven down the sides of his face deepening slightly, his light eyes twinkling with amusement – at life itself, it seemed. Standing in the waves now, cigar clamped between his teeth, he looked mischievous and anarchic, like some distant cousin of Poseidon, ruling his patch of sea.

'Thank you,' I said, diving back into the water.

As the sun lowered on the horizon, spattering the sea with its golden, trembling reflection, the butler and the maid trudged down the path to the beach lugging a large wicker basket, each of them holding a handle, faces flushed. Inside the basket, bottles clinked against one another promisingly. Several other guests had joined us for predinner drinks. All of them cheered as the butler arrived. 'Hurrah for Jerzi!' they cried. The gloomy butler allowed the corners of his mouth to turn up very slightly at this welcome. Guests hurled orders at him as he unpacked the full bar.

'Ask him anything,' said Herb, 'he knows it.'

'Can you make a Maiden's Prayer?' asked Trudy, the wife of Max Kessler, herself a writer, who was wearing a patterned head scarf pulled tight over her hair, her mouth a fuchsia slash. The butler nodded solemnly and took a bottle of gin out of one of the baskets, a jug of orange juice. Cointreau.

'I don't believe it!' exclaimed Trudy, sipping the drink, her eyes closed with pleasure.

'And what about Pippa Sarkissian?' asked Herb. 'What would she like?'

'Crème de menthe,' I said.

'An old-fashioned girl, underneath it all,' said Herb, chuckling.

Gigi tossed her head. 'Crème de menthe isn't a cocktail, it's a liqueur,' she said.

Herb turned to her. 'Rubbing alcohol for you, my love?'

'A big glass, please,' said Gigi playfully, plonking herself opposite Herb with a swiveling movement, her long legs folding graciously beneath her. Somehow she had managed to change into a diaphanous coral halter dress and was fully made up. Yet I hadn't noticed her leaving. Herb took out a bottle of champagne and poured her a glass. I wondered if their corrosive banter was for real or not. Gigi drank and sighed, looking around her with half-closed eyes, like a contented lioness. The sky had begun to go pink. 'After this,' said Gigi, 'everyone can get ready for dinner and the others will arrive.'

Back in the transparent box, Craig and I walked up the metal staircase, down the hall, which was open to the rest of the house, and into our room, described to us by Gigi airily as the 'third door.' The smell of jasmine was heavy and sweet. The drapes were shut. We flicked the light switch. Two identical lamps shone a warm light on a stainless steel bed, a quilted white bedspread, embroidered linen pillowcases. And, laid out on the bed neatly, were all our clothes, our books, and, in a small Baggie, the drugs we had brought for the weekend: a handful of pills, a lump of hash, and a singed spoon, which Terry and Jed always brought with them, just in case, though neither of them was a junkie.

Craig grimaced. 'That fucking butler.'

'He's a humorist,' I said, bouncing on the bed and opening the Baggie. Craig clambered on top of me, jabbing me with his elbow. I wasn't in the right frame of mind for a big sex procedure, so I made him come with my mouth, then brushed my teeth, resolving to go to the party straight, but for one little Valium, which didn't count, it just took the edge off, made me slightly numb. I didn't want to give that nasty butler the satisfaction of being high. But also, I didn't want Herb to see me high. I didn't admit it to myself, but in the back of my mind, I was already thinking that I wanted him to like me.

Poker-faced Craig was still showering. He was intensely vain, so it always took him ages to get ready for anything. I walked downstairs alone, my steps echoing on the metal staircase. Sam Shapiro was standing beside Herb. They were looking out the immense glass wall, talking, drinks in their hands. Hearing me, they both turned and looked up.

'The artist's girlfriend,' Herb said. I was wearing an old ballet tutu with a light blue bodice and my black lace-up boots. Bright red lipstick, shiny black nails. 'Come. Talk to us.'

I sat down on the couch. Sam and Herb sat opposite me. They were looking at me as though I were a specimen from a newly discovered tribe of pygmies.

'So. Pippa,' said Herb. 'What do you normally have for breakfast?'

Sam broke into laughter, a painful, honking guffaw.

'I don't really eat breakfast,' I said.

'Does she look like she eats breakfast?' said Sam.

'Now there's your first mistake,' said Herb, wagging his finger at me paternally.

'Do you go straight into the studio, then?' asked Sam.

'I don't have a studio.'

'You must be an artist, dressed like that,' said Sam.

'No,' I said.

'What are you then?' asked Herb.

I shrugged. 'I work in a clothing store.'

'You must have some ambition,' said Herb.

'Why?' I asked him. He looked startled, as though he had noticed something odd about my face.

'Well, I congratulate you,' he said. 'You are the first person who has ever walked across the threshold of this house who isn't riddled with ambition, frustrated or otherwise. Even the butler is writing a short story. He broke the news to me yesterday.'

Gigi stormed out of the kitchen, flushed and upset. Herb stood and went to her swiftly. They conferred in whispers for a few moments. He put his hand on her shoulder. She wiped tears from her cheeks. Sam looked at me and raised his eyebrows, whispering: 'Watch out for the wife.'

The other guests trickled in over the next hour or so. Gradually, it became clear that Herb and Gigi had different tastes in people. Herb's friends were the intellectuals, an ironic, serious lot. The women, as they appeared, had no scales on their eyes and hadn't for years; they looked like they had seen it all. The men glowered at one another and huddled together, conversing intensely about matters of importance. Gigi's gang was younger, decadent. There was a theater director who arrived in a one-piece terry-cloth pantsuit; an actress who, it was whispered, had worked with

Warhol; and the maverick playboy scion of a famous record label. Craig and the rest of us had clearly been invited to tip the balance in Gigi's favor.

Once it was dark, tiny torches flickered all along the path to the beach. The house was twinkling with candlelight. I milled around, a ginger ale in my hand, listening to shards of conversation. Magnificent food was displayed on various tables. Now and then, Gigi would reach into a small drawer in the dining room table at which she and a few others were sitting with their plates and pull out a little silver bell. It made a pretty, tinkling sound. Whenever she rang it, the butler or the maid would appear, and Gigi would order another bottle of champagne, or something special that had to be concocted to order. Looking up at the maid, making a face like a hopeful child, she said, 'Alfonsa, could you please, please ask Maria if she could make me a little tiny chocolate mousse, just for a taste?' Alfonsa smiled, glancing at the elaborate desserts already piled high before her mistress, and walked off. The poor cook.

I glimpsed Herb here and there, conferring with the serious men or listening to Gigi's flamboyant guests with an alienated smile. I had the strange sensation of knowing what he was feeling; I could read his face. I could tell if he was uninterested, or impatient, or delighted. After a while, though, I lost track of him. Sam Shapiro came up to me on the porch as I sat with poker-faced Craig and Terry. The two of them were laughing, hugging, and I was wondering if they wouldn't make a nice couple. I had grown tired of Craig, with his puffy eyes and frozen face, his blond hair that stuck straight up on his head. He was the most gifted of the bunch, but he was a cold person, and in bed there was a wooden reserve in him I found dispiriting.

'Beautiful night,' said Sam. I turned to him and wondered what it would be like to kiss him. It was clear that he was wondering something along the same lines. But I found myself excusing myself in the middle of our conversation. The truth was, I thought, as

I meandered through that house, looking up into the night sky through the great glass roof, every star visible, the truth was, I didn't want anyone anymore, or anything. I wanted to sleep for seven months. I was burned out. Exhausted. Bored. I suppose I was depressed, but I didn't think about things like that in those days. There was a light on in the little yellow cottage, I noticed. I wondered if it was all right to walk inside, or if that was Gigi and Herb's private domain, the place where they played out their mysterious relationship. The door was slightly ajar. I peeked through the window. The TV was on; a football match was playing. Men in helmets tumbled over one another, landing in a pile. On the couch, his arms spread over the back, was Herb. I opened the door and walked in.

He looked up. When he saw it was me, his face creased into a smile. 'Just the girl I want to see,' he said. 'You like football?'

'I used to – I have four brothers.'

'Have a seat. Refresh your memory.' We sat watching the game for a few minutes. I snuck a look at his profile. His Roman nose and high forehead, the thick, silver hair rising from his face like a wave, made him look like an emperor. I had never seen a man who exuded such authority. He offered me pistachio nuts and a Coke from a little fridge near the TV.

'This is the most amazing house I've ever seen,' I said.

'It's not a house, it's a hellhole,' said Herb. 'Not one comfortable piece of furniture, except this couch. It's like living in an aquarium.'

'Why do you live here then?'

'My wife,' he said, with a gesture encompassing the cottage, the house, the sea beyond. 'I couldn't afford to live like this. Not that I'm a poor man.' We watched another play. When the commercial came on, he turned to me. 'So, little Pippa,' he said. 'Don't you think it's time to change your life?'

'What do you mean?'

'Doesn't it get dispiriting to be so aimless? I mean, I see that you're young, but a person of such unusual sweetness –'

'I'm not sweet.'

'People can be experienced and sweet. I'm talking about an innate quality. It's a long time since I've seen it in a person.' I was shocked to feel tears well up in my eyes. Herb was sweeping my face with his gaze, as though he were hungry for my emotion. Just then, the door swung open, and Gigi ran to Herb, giggling, and pulled him off the couch. The party was going to the beach. 'Andiamo!' She led him off by his long arms, and he trotted out of the room awkwardly, like a goat walking on its hind legs.

Everyone skipped or ran or shuffled to the beach. I broke up with Craig with quiet brutality on the way down the path. I explained that I needed a hiatus from romance. Not that our relationship was romantic. He was slightly morose after that, but Terry did her best to comfort him, and within half an hour he was stripping with the rest of my friends. It looked like a bluefish feed, all those people, some buck naked, some half-clothed, chopping up the water. I remained dressed and thought about sharks. I was feeling somber. Something had stirred in me. About five yards away, I saw Herb, also dressed, watching his wife as she frolicked in a bra and panties, looking like Aphrodite born out of the sea complete with lingerie. I had never seen such a perfectly formed woman. When I looked back at Herb, he was turned in my direction. I couldn't tell for sure, but I thought he was staring at me.

The next morning, we all played tennis. It was Craig and I against Gigi and Jed. Herb stood by and watched, a towel draped around his neck. He had already played singles with Sam Shapiro. Gigi threw herself into the game. Whenever she scored, she jumped into the air, elated. When she missed the ball, she ran to Herb, ducking her head into his chest. At one point, after missing two shots in a row, she let her racket clatter onto the court, turned, and ran off toward the house. Herb didn't miss a beat. He ambled on with his loose-limbed gait, picked up his wife's racket, and served.

*

Back on Orchard Street, Terry was now shacked up with poker-faced Craig, so I got her room, which she had painted puce in a fit of jealousy years before I was adopted into the group. In the old, Jewish days of the Lower East Side, this loft had been devoted to the manufacture of ladies' girdles and crammed, no doubt, with hollow-eyed women and children, sewing their lives away elbow to elbow for a starving wage. But times had changed. The neighborhood was now given over to longtime Hispanic residents, a few artists desperate for cheap rent, and of course the junkies.

When they found the place, Jed and Craig and Calvin put up the Sheetrock walls themselves, creating a space with several bedrooms and studios. The tall, dusty windows let in plenty of light. The place was bright but filthy, with a damp towel perpetually drooped over the glass door of the jerry-rigged shower stall, hair wound around the creviced bar of yellowing soap. The kitchen was in the hall and consisted of a hot plate set on top of a small refrigerator. When you walked barefoot, you got sawdust on your feet. The air smelled of cigarettes, oil paint, and the polyurethane that Jed used to laminate his sculptures: stuffed animals set into elaborate, upholstered frames skillfully painted in the style of Tiepolo. My clothes and hair reeked of this cocktail of odors.

Since the most recent change of romantic alliance, Craig was a little bit reserved with me. I think he was sore about the abrupt breakup on the way to the beach at Gigi and Herb's house. Usually, our transfers were more seamless and unspoken, less like the ending of a regular couple. Perhaps he was insulted by my pedestrian technique, which implied he gave a shit, which of course he didn't. Jed and Calvin were both expecting me to move over in bed for one or the other of them, as I normally would have, but I was too tired. The week after we got back from Herb and Gigi's house, I slept most of the time when I wasn't at work. I think maybe I was trying to avoid my next boyfriend. I slept so deeply over those few days, it felt like I might just float away in some dream and die.

When Herb called me, it was one o'clock in the afternoon, I didn't have to be at work till nine. No one else was in the loft, the answering machine was off, the phone kept ringing and ringing. Finally I staggered out of my room and dropped to the floor as I answered, leaning against the wall, whispering 'Hulluh' and struggling to light a cigarette I'd found in a crushed pack under the table. My neck was clammy, eyes unfocused. I was almost incoherent with sleep. He asked me out for breakfast. Even half-conscious, I knew that I shouldn't go out with him, so very married as he was, but I hadn't been able to get him out of my mind ever since he'd told me I was sweet. To prove him wrong, perhaps, I saw him.

He treated me like a pal. He was avuncular. He filled me with eggs and coffee, teased me about being a waster. I called him an old fart. We saw each other plenty after that. We would weave around the city, laughing and talking. He found me amusing. I found him reassuring. Once, we walked all the way up Madison Avenue. He led me into a really expensive store and made me try on this black cocktail dress. The cloth was cool and smooth against my skin. It made me look shockingly pretty. I took it off. Then, while I was dreamily sliding silk coats along their rack like the beads of an abacus, he bought me the dress. He bought me shoes, too, very high, pointy heels with straps around the ankles. I knew I shouldn't accept these things, and the truth was I found them slightly ridiculous. They were too on-the-nose sexy for the taste I'd learned back at the loft – not enough irony, not enough edge. Yet wearing them thrilled me. Gigi was away in Italy at the time. Herb asked me if I would come over for dinner.

The small elevator reeked of gardenia perfume, with an undertone of fried garlic. I sat down on the leather bench. It felt cool against the backs of my thighs, which were bare because I was wearing the cocktail dress Herb had given me. I pulled the old cardigan I was wearing around me and looked up at the walls, which were upholstered in heavy, amethyst-colored linen. I was just imagining moving into the elevator – where would I put the bed, the sink, a little carpet – when the doors opened right into Herb's apartment. And there was Herb, his emperor's face creased into a smile, his long arms open.

'Beautiful,' he proclaimed. I tottered out of the elevator in the massive heels he'd bought me that afternoon. He gave me a hug. He was wearing a soft brown sweater. It felt like a rabbit. He smelled like limes. When he let go, I looked around. It was an old apartment, he said. Built before the Second World War. Gigi had decorated the place in red and blue and yellow. 'It's a bit like a home for disturbed children,' said Herb.

We sat down on either end of the poppy-red couch, bashful now that we were alone in his apartment. A large Yves Klein painting with imprints of naked women in blue paint on raw canvas hung on the wall opposite us. Herb went into the kitchen and came out with a bottle of champagne. We drank. I was so hungry; I felt the alcohol behind my eyes immediately. I imagined what Suky would think if she saw me now, sipping champagne in *costly garments*, as she used to say. What a mix of excitement and jealousy would be sloshing around inside her. I finished my glass, and he poured me another, brought out a bag of potato chips.

'I let the maid go home, so I'm afraid it's just me tonight. You won't have the service you deserve.'

'That's okay,' I said. All I could think about was his broad trunk, the reassuring baritone of his voice, the way his corduroys fit him so loosely, Mr Brown had worn pants like that. Was that why I was here? I wondered. Because of a pair of corduroys? All of a sudden, I was overcome with sleepiness and wanted to lie down. I ate a handful of chips. 'Dinner's almost ready,' he said, standing up. 'Don't despair.'

The dining room was all white: Lucite table, marble floor, translucent plastic chairs, crystal chandelier. Herb pulled my chair out, then put a big glass bowl of pasta with tomato sauce between us. 'I hope the sauce is okay,' he said. 'I haven't cooked anything since I was thirty.' It was the best food I had ever tasted. I ate like I was starving. He put more in my bowl. 'So, Pippa. Shall I tell you some of the things I like about you?'

'Okay,' I said, my mouth full of spaghetti.

'Well, let's see. You're not a show-off, but I think you're damn smart. You've got an original way of living, for this town. You're in it for the experience, is that right?' He made being utterly lost sound like a good thing. 'You're beautiful, but you're cool about it. You don't even seem to know how lovely you are. And . . . I don't know, I suppose there's sadness there, and I like sadness. In moderation.'

'I like your corduroys,' I said.

'Is that it?'

'No. I like your face. Your voice. I . . . This is going to sound weird.'

'Say.'

'It's like I feel what you're feeling. If you're feeling sad, or nervous, or happy – I feel it in my body, in my fingers.'

'What a remarkable thing.' He sat and looked at me for a moment. Then he said, 'I don't ever want you to have to censor yourself around me. I want to know you, Pippa. I want to know who you are. Tell me one thing about yourself. The most important thing.'

I thought about that for a while. Then I took off my cardigan, stood up, took my pasta bowl, set it on the cold marble floor beside his chair, went down on all fours in my finery, and ate out of the bowl like a dog. I knew he could see the marks Shelly and Kat had left on my back. I have never felt so naked, before or since. After a few seconds, he gripped me around the waist, lifted me onto his lap, dipped his napkin in his water glass, and washed off my face. His eyes were glistening. 'No, no, no,' he said. 'I don't believe it. Who did this to you?'

He carried me into a bedroom. It was not his room – he told

me it was not his room. He said I was a queen. 'I don't know who put this spell on you, darling. But if I'm good for anything, it's to show you how wonderful you are.' When he put his hand on my abdomen, I felt a sudden, deep, pulsing ache, not pain but desire, desire in my womb. That's the only way I can describe it. I was so wet it soaked through my dress onto the sheets. That was the first night I really made love. It wasn't my pleasure and his pleasure, a transaction – 'and here's your change, ma'am' – it was just wordless, thoughtless, and complete, like two waves crashing together and becoming the same water.

And that's how we buried Gigi Lee, kicked the sand over her perfect body with our bare feet as we wriggled toward each other in her very own guest bed.

Kept

Herb rented me a studio apartment on Seventieth and Lexington in a building with shining brass doors and a doorman called Nathan. I felt like an alien uptown; I was dressed wrong for everything, even buying milk. But Herb came over with something new for me to wear every few days, until I didn't feel dressed wrong anymore. I just felt like I was impersonating somebody else. Herb picked me up every afternoon at my new job in a fancy shoe store on Madison Avenue and walked me up to my little apartment. The walls were stark bluish white. There was a pine table in the kitchen, a black couch in the living room. I kept the place immaculate. I wanted it to be blank, a place for a person to change into another person. I took no pills. I got into no trouble. Herb said I was his true wife; he had found me at last.

When he told me, I was thrilled, incredulous, laughing. 'What are you, fucking crazy? That's the last thing you need.'

'I see something in you,' he said, looking at me steadily and sweeping the hair from my eyes. 'Something you don't see.'

'Anyway,' I said somberly. 'You have a wife.'

He threw himself back on the pillows. 'If I have to live with that lunatic one more week, I'll hang myself. For years I've been hoping she'll have an affair so I can get out of it. But she won't do it. The bitch.'

I yearned to say yes, but I was scared of Gigi, and I was afraid of what I would do to Herb. I hurt everyone I loved, everyone I met, practically. How could I trust myself with marriage?

153

Pivot

The doorbell rang, which was a bad sign. I hadn't ordered take-out, Herb had keys. No one else knew where I was. I said 'Hello' and heard Gigi's voice. Fright flashed through my wrists. I said I was on my way down. I thought I would be safer on the street. Just as I was pulling on my jacket, there was a knock on the door. I contemplated running down the fire escape, but then I opened the door. There she was, looking over-the-top gorgeous, like something out of *La Dolce Vita*, a black dress and a fur coat, long dark hair and bangs, that drooping, voluptuous mouth, mascara bleeding around her tragic eyes. She walked around the place on stiletto heels without saying anything, looked the kitchen over, stalked into the bedroom, the bathroom. Then she stood there and took me in. I was in a tank top and sweatpants, my stringy hair scraped back in a ponytail. I looked like I should be her masseuse or maybe her tennis coach, but not her replacement. No way. 'You whore,' she said. That was nice.

'I'm not a whore,' I said.

'Is not a whore paid for sex? What do you call this? I knew it the minute I laid eyes on you. I knew you were no good – a predator, and the worst kind, the unconscious kind. Things just "happen" to you, don't they? And before you know it you steal my husband!'

I tried to check inside her open coat for a weapon. I thought if she was unarmed, I could defend myself. 'I'm sorry,' I said.

'He told me he loves you,' she said.

I don't know how she ended up clutching my knees. I looked down, and she was kneeling, her coat splayed out behind her like the train of a dwarf queen. 'You can stay here, see him, have a love affair, but do not take him, please, don't take him –'

I don't remember what I said. It was something like 'Okay, I won't,' I think, because she was out of there like a puff of smoke.

I couldn't make love to Herb after that. I knew I should move out, but I really didn't have enough money for a security deposit anyplace unless I found a roommate, and I didn't know anyone anymore. I couldn't go back to Jim or Trish or Suky or the loft. I mean, I could have gone back, but I knew it would lead to disaster. Herb was very understanding. He insisted I stay in the apartment on my own, even though that meant he had to stay in a hotel, because it was so painful to be with Gigi, now that she knew. He called and told me he loved me ten times a day, sent me flowers, sent me a necklace. I didn't want to talk to him. When I came home from work, I just curled up in bed and tried not to think about getting high. There was a Catholic church down the street, and, though I was not Catholic, I went there often. Not for Mass so much, just to sit there and pray and ask forgiveness over and over and over. All I ever did was cause misery and distress, and I was still doing it. I wrote my parents a note to say I was well and had a place and please don't worry and I think it's probably best I stay out of the way from now on, given the circumstances. I didn't intend to put a return address on the envelope, but then I did.

*

One morning, Herb let himself into the apartment, dragged me out of bed, dressed me, stuffed me into his Jaguar, and drove me to his beach house just so I could take a walk on the sand, breathe in the sea air. As we drove up to that glass-encased dollhouse, I was deluged with feeling for Herb, the same heady certainty that had gripped me when I watched him at Gigi's party: that I knew him, understood him, craved his company. So it was very smart of him to bring me back there.

On the way home, it was night. We were on a narrow country road. Herb's headlights raked a little fawn on the side of the road.

Its legs were folded up underneath its body, and it had its ears pricked up. Herb pulled the car over. We got out. As we approached, we could see that the creature was frightened, trembling, but it didn't run; drew its ears back and bowed its head. 'Maybe his mother got hit by a car,' I said.

'His legs are broken,' Herb said. 'Otherwise he would have run away.'

'Should we bring him to a vet?' I asked. Herb lifted up the fawn's body. Its two hind legs dangled, useless and bloody; its front legs made a pathetic galloping motion in the air.

'They can't help him,' he said.

'We can't just leave him here,' I said.

Herb gently laid the deer back on the ground and got back in the car. I sat next to him. He was silent for a long time. He took in a long breath, let it out again. 'Close your eyes and cover your ears,' he said.

'Why?' I asked.

'Just do it,' he said. He backed up the car about five yards. Through the windshield, I watched the fawn, frosted ghostly white by the headlights. Herb put the car into gear, stepped on the accelerator. I screamed, but he didn't swerve. I squeezed my eyes tight, felt the thud as we hit the deer. The car had stopped. Herb backed up, got out, checked to see that it was dead. Then he steered the car back onto the road and drove us to the city.

We didn't speak on the ride home. When he stopped outside my building, he looked at me. 'It would have starved or frozen or been devoured,' he said. 'You know that?'

I nodded. He slept at my place that night. Very early in the morning, I was woken by the sound of him weeping. I turned him over, wiped his tears away. I loved him then. To have the courage to do something that hurt you so much. A strange act of kindness. It was then that I knew, absolutely. 'I will marry you,' I said.

'You will?' He sounded baffled.

'How could I not?'

Bullet

Herb called me from a phone booth on Park Avenue.

'I told her we're getting married.'

'How was it?'

'Horrible, and then . . . slightly less horrible.'

'Come home, then,' I said. He did. We scrambled eggs, toasted bagels, watched bad TV in bed till three in the morning. We were so happy.

'You need to be a little careful,' Herb said, 'about Gigi.'

'What do you mean, she's going to try and kill me?'

'No, no, no. But she's volatile. And feeling scorned. So if the buzzer rings and you're alone here, don't answer.'

'What if I ordered in?'

'Don't order in unless I'm here.'

A few weeks went by. Herb gradually moved his things over: boxes of books, a couple of framed posters of old films, and his limited but high-quality wardrobe. The divorce papers were being drawn up. Gigi stayed away. We lived inside a little nutshell of contentment. We saw almost no one. Only Sam Shapiro, Herb's trusted ally, was allowed in on our secret. A couple of times a week, the three of us would go out, and Sam would regale us with stories about his disastrous love life, or gripe about his new novel.

One such night, Sam got to the apartment before Herb did. He sat back on the ink black couch sipping a glass of pineapple juice, watching shivering saffron squares of sunlight appear and disappear on the wall as the sun set. His young, taut, raptor face shone with humor and curiosity. 'Don't you have any hooch?' he asked me.

159

'Nope,' I said. 'But I could make you a sandwich.'

'You sure have cleaned up your act,' he said, looking over at me skeptically.

I laughed. 'You don't believe it?'

'There are two schools of thought regarding change in human beings. Yes, and no.'

'What do you think?'

'Fundamentally . . . no. But I hope I'm wrong. For my own sake.' His ironic tone was shot through with wistfulness.

'What would you change about yourself if you could?' I asked softly, leaping, I knew, forward, toward him.

He thought for a few seconds. 'I would be less of an observer. I'm sick of being the specter at the feast. You see, Pippa, I'm one of those unlucky beings who don't fully exist. I live off other people. But all writers are vampires, hasn't Herb told you that?'

'Not yet.'

'If I find the right girl, she'll make me real.'

'Do you really believe that?'

'*You're* real.' He looked at me then with genuine longing. The shape of our narrative could have melted then and there; Herb might have come home to two young people falling in love. But I didn't topple. I really had changed, I realized. I wasn't going to seduce or be seduced anymore. Not even by this ravenous creature here, tempting as it was to evoke some actual passion from his ever-watchful, ever-thinking being. I looked away and stood up, aware of something having shifted inside me, some internal door closing. I had been tamed at last.

'So, Dracula, am I gonna end up in one of your books now? The little fuckup who went straight?' I asked.

'I don't think you'd fit into any of the stories in my head,' he said, back to his usual, arch tone.

'How come?'

'You're too . . . I don't know, really. I was going to say primitive, but that's not it. That sad little smile, but you really do enjoy

160

life. Winsome but naughty – you're an ingenue femme fatale – oddly calm, almost remote . . . You're hard to put a finger on, Pippa.' He smiled at his own pun.

That night, in the cab going downtown, and sitting in the movie theater, I felt especially safe, wedged between these two men, protected by their solicitude and desire. Herb took Sam's crush as a compliment to him. It didn't bother him in the slightest. We all knew I was Herb's girl.

Then, one day, the phone rang. Herb answered. 'Hi,' he said, surprised, anxious. He listened for a long time, interjected little. When he hung up, he said, 'Isn't that the most extraordinary thing.'

'What?'

'Gigi wants us to go out to the beach house for lunch.'

'Why?'

'She wants us to come and make the switch there.'

'*Make the switch?*'

'She wants to be civilized, she wants to be sophisticated and show she doesn't mind losing me. I don't know.'

'You mean you want to *go*? What happened to not answering the door in case she sticks a knife in my chest?'

'No, no, her voice was totally different. Calm. Gigi has a rational side, it kicks in at the damnedest times.' He shook his head, chuckling. 'I'll bet you she has a man. That has to be it. She's going to unveil him at this lunch. Everything is about vanity for Gigi.'

So, the following Saturday, we drove to the beach. The glass casing of the house glared in the sun. Inside it, the quaint little cottage looked like it was on display in a museum of the future. Beside it, there might have been a sign reading: 'This is a reconstruction of an early-twentieth-century dwelling, complete with art and cooking implements.' Herb sprang out of the car. I stayed in my seat as though magnetized, my limbs leaden. The skin on my face felt heavy, like clay. I was becoming very sleepy.

Herb's tread on the gravel sounded brisk, optimistic. I heard the trunk click open. I opened the door, stuck my head out, and looked back at him, trying to see what he was doing.

'Can I go to the beach for a while?' I asked. I thought if I lay down in the sand, I might get my strength back. I could see only the top of Herb's face; the lid of the trunk obscured the rest. When he slammed it shut, he was holding his tennis racket. He was grabbing on to Gigi's offer of a conciliatory lunch a little desperately, I thought. He just couldn't resist the idea of a civilized finish to his second marriage. His first, dissolved acrimoniously over thirty years ago, he dismissed as the bloodless coupling of two neophyte intellectuals who mistook a shared passion for *Also Sprach Zarathustra* for love.

Just as Herb was about to answer me, Gigi came out of the house. The light breeze molded the fine cloth of her orange caftan to her statuesque form, making her look like a bustier version of the Winged Venus. She held out her arms, then thought better of it and put her hands on her hips. 'Welcome,' she said. Now I really had to get out of the car.

We walked into the house. The sweet, full smell of jasmine hit me like heat, seeped into my brain, and conjured up a memory of my first visit – the sight of Herb and Gigi on the beach, the sweet iced tea, the brief sense of ownership I'd felt when I looked down at the sea from the porch. Let's face it: I had coveted Gigi's life at that moment. It wasn't the money – no, not exactly that. It was just that the money made everything seem all right. It made you feel safe. The smell of fresh flowers in a guest room. The taste of iced tea made by someone else. It was the opposite of chaos, the opposite of everything I had known until that time. I wanted to be sheltered at last. Yes, I confess: I wanted what Gigi had, and in a blind, unthinking, but ruthless way, I set about getting it.

As we entered, Jerzi the butler gave Herb a look of the darkest humor, his eyelids drooping, face impassive, one eyebrow raised. Herb shrugged and allowed himself to smile slightly. Seated in the glacial white leather couch was Sam Shapiro, looking awkward and surprised. I turned to Herb, who greeted his tense young friend with a hearty handshake, a quizzical look on his face. Could Sam be sleeping with Gigi? That would be too neat. Yet the way she let her fingers linger on Sam's hand when she passed him a drink, her stage whisper for him to get the cheese and salami out of the kitchen, when Alfonsa would be doing it in moments – it was all adding up. Herb paid special attention to Sam, slapping him on the back and asking him how his novel was going, when he had spoken to him the day before on that very subject, just to let him know it was okay if he *was* sleeping with his soon to be ex-wife.

Gigi hadn't managed to look at me directly. She was all smiles and bustle, flushed and seemingly happy to be doing this highly original thing. Yet there was something acted about her movements, gestures, expressions, as if she was imitating herself. I was filled with unease. Herb was grinning, teeth clenched, determined to get through this ordeal so he could have what he wanted. Sam looked like he wanted to disappear. The little ocher cottage in the center of the room had its white shades drawn demurely, as if lowering its eyes in embarrassment. It occurred to me that I hadn't really spoken yet. In fact, no dialogue seemed required of me in this play we were all enacting. It was more than enough for me to simply exist. I was, after all, the reason we were all here, in this new configuration. I needed no more lines than Helen of Troy. Pippa the Destroyer.

Champagne was poured; we each drank a glass. Gigi poured Herb a second glass, glancing up at him with impish insouciance, her tiny nose retreating into her face as it did when she was about to smile but didn't. Was it possible that she was flirting with him? The champagne left a dull weight on my forehead. Again, I wanted to lie down, to sleep, to be gone. I wished they could do it all without me. Alfonsa was looking worried as she put the finishing touches on the table set for four. She kept changing the location of the butter dish, the saltcellar, her eyes traveling back and forth over the table as if she were speed-reading. 'You can bring in the food now, Alfonsa,' said Gigi, gently chiding, as though encouraging a forgetful child. She ushered us out onto the porch with a sweep of her arm. 'Take a few breaths before we eat,' she said.

'There's oxygen in here, too,' said Herb, adopting his old teasing way with her. Gigi giggled, and for a moment I thought it was all going to unravel; we would drop the scene as written, go back to our old parts. Herb and Gigi: worldly married couple; me: adoptive waif kept around as a decent-looking pet, a sort of representative of the Order of Flotsam; Sam: the brilliant friend who haunted his own life like a ghost, hunted down by his talent and sheltered, as I was, in the home of two knowing benefactors. I almost wished it were true. It would have been safer that way. I looked at Herb. He seemed impossibly old, from another world. I wanted him to hold me, to break through this web I was weaving around myself, to make us real again.

Gigi went into the house to check on the food. We all sighed at once.

'Well, this is one odd situation,' said Sam.

'Sorry you got roped into it,' said Herb.

'I didn't know it was happening till you drove up,' said Sam.

'Listen, it's a load off my mind,' said Herb, putting his hand between my shoulder blades.

'What is?' asked Sam.

'You and Gigi.'

'*What?* She invited me over to lunch! That's *it!*'

'That's what *you* say,' said Herb, smiling slightly at Sam's new predicament.

Sam looked over at me appreciatively and shook his head. 'The mystery girl,' he said.

Gigi opened the glass doors then and ushered us in. Our repast was laid out on the table like a grim offering to some vengeful god. A severed calf's head stared out at us mournfully; a leathery suckling pig had its mouth stretched wide, a too-big apple stuffed into it. Between these monstrosities, a bowl of perfectly browned potatoes and glistening salad seemed like no-man's-land.

'This lunch is in honor of telling it like it is,' said Gigi, seating Herb to her right, Sam to her left, and me across from her. Herb was on edge now; I could feel it. 'You know, how we all eat chops and things and we don't think of the faces, of who gets killed.'

'It's lucky no one's a vegetarian,' Herb said.

'In America,' Gigi said, 'you are very realistic. I mean to say, grand gestures have no place for you. Here is the truth as I see it. A pig for a cow. A fair exchange.'

'Who's who?' Sam couldn't help asking.

Gigi shrugged, tears in her eyes.

'Sorry,' said Sam, staring into his plate.

'Let's just have lunch,' said Herb in a subdued tone, picking up a carving knife. 'Who wants pig?'

'First,' said Gigi, 'a toast.' She raised her wine. Sunlight streamed through the glass wall behind her and glinted off the crystal; a star of light exploded out of her hand. 'To transformation,' she said. We all raised our glasses dutifully, drank. Then she opened the little drawer in the table, the secret little drawer where she kept her bell, and took out a shiny, black thing, no bigger than a mouse. It was hard and perfect in the palm of her hand.

'Gigi,' said Herb, standing up. 'Give me that thing.' He reached out. 'Give it to me.' She smiled up at him, a strange smile of satiation, of victory. 'Isn't it funny,' she said, 'how men always marry women who are easier and easier to dominate, until they end up with an imbecile?' Sam sat rigid, his face pale with terror. Gigi rested her elbow on the table, her wrist slack, the little black gun dangling in her hand like the droopy head of a fading flower. Then she turned to me. I waited for the bullet. I wondered if it would be in my chest, my head. I saw myself running to the door, shot in the back. Her eyes on mine, she parted her lips as if to speak, and wedged the tiny gun into her mouth. Herb lunged for

165

her, grabbing her shoulder as the shell exploded. As he pulled her toward him, her head dropped to the table, and a fine spray of blood the shape of a huge Japanese fan surged out of her serpentine black hair, spattering him, all of us, like lava shooting out of an angry volcano. The glass behind her was coated ruby red. Herb was bent over his wife as if petrified, his face covered in blood. Alfonsa was screaming, running back and forth senselessly. With horrible slowness, the body slipped from the table, the chair, then flopped bonelessly to the floor.

I turned then and ran out of that bloody glass box, through the French doors, onto the porch, down the rotting wooden stairs, following the narrow path, the branches of the scrub pine snagging my dress like clawing hands. I staggered onto the beach; the sand tripped me up, it felt thick as towels. I flicked my shoes off so I could keep running, the hot sand searing the soles of my feet, and fled into the cool sea. All I remember is wanting to go under, far under, into the darkest, most frigid part of the water, where I could wash the blood off. I think I was screaming; a man came running toward me, a white dog by his side. After I went under, he pulled me to the surface and asked me what had happened as the dog paddled desperately beside me, barking. I couldn't answer him. What *had* happened? Was it a suicide, or was it a murder? And if it was a murder, who did it?

Home

A month before the wedding, Herb convinced me to invite my parents. He thought if they weren't there, the marriage might not seem as real to me. I hadn't spoken to Suky in years. I had cut her off completely, and, though I thought she was secretly grateful for it, initially I still dreamed that she would find me somehow, turn up at my apartment clear eyed and dope free, ready to go shopping, or out for a milk shake. But it didn't happen that way. Any news I had from the family came in the form of fact-filled letters from my father, who told me of all the plumbing and boiler repairs, my brothers' exploits, and other local items of interest. They always ended with 'Your mother sends you her love.' This sentence read like a taunt; Suky had made her choice, and she hadn't chosen me. Kat's advice, to forget the past, to look ahead, only ahead, turned out to be very effective in the long run. Gradually I stopped crying about my mother. I bled the emotion from her memory until it hung lifeless in my mind, like a pig on a hook in a butcher shop window.

My oldest brother, Chester, called me every now and then to make sure I was all right, and we met in the city occasionally. Sometimes he gave me a little money. After I disappeared, Chester had gone to medical school. He was a doctor now. He still had the somber, disaffected delivery of his youth, but now it made him seem authoritative, a man you could trust. I was surprised to hear his voice when I finally got up the courage to call my parents' house.

'She's in no shape to go to a wedding,' he said.

'What do you mean?' I asked.

'She's sick.'

'Sick how?'

'It's complicated.'

Herb and I drove up to Connecticut the next weekend. Des did what he could to discourage me from coming, but now I had to see her. As we drove up to the Green, I noticed that the paint on the house was flaking off. I wondered when my father would have to retire. We rang the bell at the front door, which felt odd; I had never used the front door growing up. But I was a stranger now. Chester came to greet us. I hugged him. Behind him, Des stood, smaller now, it seemed, the pouches under his eyes reddish, his hair gray. He had always been a calm man, but now he seemed resigned. He kissed me on the part of my hair and led me into the living room.

She was sitting on her favorite little armchair, in a quilted pink bed jacket and a dress so big for her it looked like it belonged to someone else. She had shrunk to a sliver of her former size. Always petite, she was tiny now, a wilted little thing with ankles like wrists, her thinning Lucille Ball hair pulled back in a neat ponytail, eyes glittering. She looked like an object to me. My mother was nowhere. Herb was shocked, I could tell. It took a lot to knock the wind out of his general air of removed amusement; Suky did it without trying.

She smiled politely as we walked in. Her teeth had been capped. 'Would you like some tea, you two?' It was still that voice, that high, squeaky southern voice, with a slight whistle from the foreign teeth. The twitch in her cheek had become a violent, spastic tug. I felt like running away.

'I would love some,' Herb said. He sat on the edge of the sofa and admired Suky's home. She beamed at him graciously as Chester poured the tea, then trembled uncontrollably as she tried to take a sip. Herb turned to Des and asked him about the real estate prices in the area. Had they gone up? How much? And his parish? Shrinking? Growing. How interesting. They kept that conversation up for about five minutes. Then, there was a pause.

'I have been very lucky,' Suky said. 'I have four wonderful children.'

'Five, Mom,' said Chester.

'Five children,' said Suky in mock disbelief. 'What was I thinking?' Then she chuckled, looking at me, I thought, with a sly expression entirely devoid of warmth. It seemed impossible that she no longer loved me. I had been the passion of her life! Was it possible that I looked as empty of meaning to her as she did to me? Where the hell was she? Where was my mother? I was leaking tears through the whole visit, but no one seemed to notice, and I rubbed them away like itches in the corners of my eyes.

Later, as Des helped her upstairs for her nap, Herb and I stood in the front hall to wave her off, as though she were boarding the *Queen Mary*. Halfway through her slow ascent, she stopped, her back very straight. Des looked at her expectantly. I knew she would turn around and look at me. She had to. And when she did, a shard of feeling, sharp as glass, cut through her absent stare and pierced my heart. I wanted to run up the stairs and hug her that minute. My muscles began to move. But something stayed me. I couldn't do it. The moment passed. She turned and made her way up the rest of the stairs, Des holding her wasted arm with the tips of his fingers, as if it were the fine stalk of an orchid.

Back in the living room, I slumped down on the couch, my legs weak. Chester told us in hushed tones that he was injecting her with small amounts of amphetamine combined with vitamins every few hours. The injections were keeping her alive at this point. She had been starving herself for years, he said ruefully, shaking his head. I thought about fat Grandma Sally. And about Suky, always standing by the stove eating a cup of rice pudding, never sitting with us at the table for a more than a few minutes. She started taking the drug so she wouldn't want to eat, so she would have all that energy, so she could be the perfect mother, the perfect wife. Then the drug became her personality. And I had been so mean to her.

I would come back next week, I told myself. I would come back and sit with her and talk about this and that. I would hug her then. I just hadn't been ready yet. It wasn't the right time. As it turned out, I was so busy with planning the wedding, I had to put off my visit. I never saw her again. She was dead within a month, found lying on her bed, I am told, a plate of uneaten toast perched on her sunken belly. And now, if I could have one thing, one single thing, I would ask for an afternoon with my mother. I would like to let her know how much she is loved, in spite of everything, because of everything. I would like the chance to be kind.

Novice

My wedding dress was very light pink. I thought of it as white, with one drop of Gigi's blood in it. In the photographs of our wedding day, I look like a child beside him. We were married in a church. I can still smell the dust in the air, see it swirling in the orange and blue light filtered through the circular stained-glass window behind the cross. I felt like a novice taking my vows. Marrying Herb was a new skin on me, my last chance at goodness. I knew if I fucked this up, I would be fallen forever.

Early Days

In the seven years Gigi had been married to Herb, she had never bothered to change her will; upon her demise, her millions reverted to her parents and their Italian pharmaceutical empire. Herb was both relieved and puzzled to learn this. It would, of course, have been outrageous for him to inherit his spurned wife's fortune – yet why had she never changed her will? 'She was always paranoid' was Herb's answer. Maybe she'd been right to be.

Not one of Herb's friends abandoned him after Gigi killed herself. Only her own old cronies, a handful of Europeans whom Herb had always deemed too boring or pretentious to socialize with, stayed away from him now – not that they were missed.

Just about everyone Herb knew had thought that Gigi was a head case, as it turned out, and, though all of them saw what had happened as a tragedy, they were also relieved that Herb was no longer encumbered by an erratic and increasingly embarrassing wife. What they thought of me – Well, they folded me in, like raisins in a cake recipe that doesn't call for them but won't be ruined by them, either. Herb could have married a llama and his circle would have accepted it. He was a truly charismatic man. He had some power in the publishing world, but it was his dynamic charm, his ferocious appetite for existence, his connection to a bigger, Titanic, preneurotic period in American literary life, when people drank Scotch with dinner and wrote unapologetic sentences and ruined each other's lives unconsciously, with the ignorance of children, that held people in his sway.

I clutched at marriage, held it like an infant, fed it, pampered it. No man was loved the way Herb was. He marveled at the genius of his choice as I fetched him his slippers, massaged his temples with scented oil, spent half the day cooking. I did not yet know how to truly be this new person. I did not know how to run a house, take care of a man, be faithful. But, like a dancer learning a new routine, I relied on repetition to teach my brain. At first I was lost in my role, feeling like an impostor as I forged checks with my new name, chose a décor for our new apartment, sold the house in a house and found a humbler place farther inland for weekends. I didn't really know how to shop for clothes or plan a dinner party. I just kept pretending, kept playing dress-up, answering the phone in a singsong voice, as I had when I was ten and married to my invisible husband Joey. I worked at my new identity for years, until the motions of everyday life as Herb's wife were as natural to me as walking.

It wasn't until I became pregnant with the twins, though, that I really believed my own act. These two creatures squirming inside me were facts. They had blood, eyes, destinies. Unlike me, they were born perfect, male and female, complete. I thought there was something magical about boy-girl twins. It was a gift, a sign. I gave myself to them with the joy of a penitent. And gradually, through the nights lying awake between Ben and Grace as they clutched at my hair in their sleep with their warm, soft hands, sniffed my neck, held me fast with their chubby arms, strong legs clamped over my abdomen, I began to change in a deeper way. My children's limbs grew around me like roots; I became a part of them. I began to want what I felt they needed. Using Suky as an inverse model, I made myself eat proper meals, seldom drank, took no medication.

As the twins grew up, it became clear that they had opposite personalities. Ben was kind, curious, intelligent. He loved all sports, was a good student, worked after school in the mail room of Herb's publishing house by the time he was thirteen. He was a responsible, sensible kid.

Grace was high-strung, fierce, a leader. She had strong vigilante tendencies, which became troublingly apparent at the age of five, when she knocked a boy unconscious with a softball bat for stealing her brother's SweeTart candies. As a toddler and very young child, she refused to wear clothes. I still have a scar on my wrist from a bite she gave me while I tried to wrestle her into a party dress – we were going to a wedding. In the end, I had to hire a babysitter and leave her home, because all she would wear was a string of beads. All the combs in the house had teeth missing from ill-fated attempts at taming the thick, tangled fair hair that grew in stubborn spirals around her shining, intelligent face. Grace felt everything with almost alarming intensity. She could be so possessive of me that at times I felt her affection like a plastic bag over my face. I have to admit, my feeling for her could be just as violent, and sometimes it frightened me, because I remembered Suky and the rigid clutch of her embraces, the way she held me down to kiss me, making me laugh so hard I ended up crying, feeling crushed, feeling that she would actually kill me. With Ben, it was effortless. I adored him, he adored me, that was that. But with Grace, it was a love affair, complete with sudden flashes of dislike, tearful fights, and sweet reconciliations.

One night when Grace was eight, I spied on her. I had put the twins to bed an hour before and tiptoed up to check on them. The door was ajar, and I peeked in. Ben was fast asleep. Grace, however, had secretly put on the reading light and was dancing. Her white nightgown and crazy nest of blond hair glowed in the incandescent light. The dance was both savage and graceful. She was whispering a song, or a spell, as she whirled like a dervish, round and round, her hands carving the air into arabesques. As I watched her, spellbound, through the crack in the door, I thought, What would it take to turn this feral little creature into someone who would let herself be whipped? In that instant, I realized that all I wanted for my daughter was that she be as unlike me as possible. I had to protect her.

Silently, I walked away, stealing myself for the coming sacrifice. From that night on, I began to both keep her at arm's

175

length – trying with all my might to maintain some neutrality, force the drama out of our relationship, be as little as possible like Suky – and at the same time spoil her systematically, in a deliberate, thoughtful fashion. I discouraged her from helping in the house, pushed her to play competitive sports, encouraged her tendency to dress like a boy, play like a boy. I wanted her to be like a man – to have the expectations of a man – that sense of being heir to the world. I wanted to break the chain of servitude that linked the women in my family.

My system worked. Grace grew up with arrogance, charm, optimism, and total belief in herself. The fact that she came to despise me was a sad side effect of her upbringing, but I guess it was inevitable. She saw me as pathetic, a slave, a flop. I was at the kids' service day and night. I had no job, and very little help in the house aside from the cleaning. Throughout Grace's adolescence, I hoped the day would come when she realized what I had done for her. She would then look at me with radiant love once more, as she had that afternoon long ago, when she'd taught herself to read and asked, '*Now* do you love me more than Ben?' But that moment never came. Her need for me had evaporated.

When the twins were small, I had a recurring dream that I was served up on an enormous platter and my children ate me. They had always loved ribs; they snapped mine off with strong, greasy fingers and consumed them voraciously, with barbecue sauce. The strange thing was, I was conscious in the dream, and I was smiling. All I could think of was how much protein the kids were getting.

In spite of all my devotion in the early days of my marriage, there were moments when, like a wolf domesticated by humans, I caught a scent of my old ways and felt hemmed in. A beautiful young man walking by on the street, the sight of teenagers high in the park, sometimes threw me off balance; I could feel myself teeter on the edge of my new existence and imagined the thrill of kissing a man I barely knew, or the sharp kick of amphetamine between my eyes. But I never strayed. Herb felt the solemnity of our vows, too, but he refused to cast a shadow of guilt on the marriage, doggedly seeing Gigi's suicide as the natural, almost inevitable, flowering of her illness. He savored his second dose of fatherhood. He had failed his first kids, angry mediocrities in their thirties by now. I was his shining ticket to happiness, new life, a second chance at youth. The fact that we had built our bliss on another person's despair – we forgot it eventually. We lived as if we deserved our luck.

Miranda

Yet I was plagued by a maddening insecurity about Herb's love for me. Almost invariably, the same poisonous daydream would infuse my mind as I pushed the kids through the park in their stroller, trying to lull them to sleep after lunch. The details of the fantasy were different, but the thrust was the same: I find a letter. I find a scarf. I find a pair of underpants. I come upon Herb with his lover in our apartment. I come upon them in the beach house. I come upon them in the park while walking the twins. She is always dark, tall, buxom, more intelligent than I. I weep. I mourn. I accuse. I confront. He leaves me.

I got so involved with these scenarios of betrayal and abandonment that I barely knew where I was. One day, I was walking along in Central Park, imagining haranguing Herb as his gorgeous lover covered herself with my guest bedsheets, when a lady in her sixties approached me. 'Mrs Lee?' I looked at her, confused. She had a sharp nose, small, dark, friendly eyes. She was English. It was then I realized I had tears on my face. I smiled, embarrassed, and wiped them away. She introduced herself as Miranda Lee. Herb's first wife! She'd seen a picture of me standing with Herb at some charity event. She wanted to say hello. She had become a psychotherapist. I should have taken her card. Instead, we chatted on a park bench while the twins slept. She was an intelligent woman with a sense of humor, especially about Herb. When she mentioned him, it was with an amused, condescending expression, as though he was a naughty child. Solitude radiated from her, but it wasn't imbued with bitterness. It just seemed like a fact of her life, something she accepted, even cherished. She had made a considerable life for herself since the divorce. She had a thriving practice, two sons who were her dear friends, she had a lively social life, went to the opera.

When we parted, she said I seemed like a lovely person. And then she said, 'Take care of yourself, Pippa.' She looked me in the eye when she said that. I was flustered by her warning, and slightly insulted, for Herb, and for myself, yet what she said stayed with me. After that day, I banned the fantasy of Herb's affair from my thoughts. It took a lot of discipline, but I managed to shoo it away just about every time it started running through my mind, till eventually I kicked the habit altogether. I trained myself to trust him.

Snow

I remember one winter, at the country house of friends with
young children, everyone went tobogganing but the twins and
me. I had stayed inside with them all morning, thinking they
were too young, at two, to be on anything moving so fast. Herb
came in, though, eyes shining, cheeks flushed from the cold,
and said that the other kids in the party were having a great
time, they were just a little older than ours. Wouldn't I come
out with the twins? Herb rarely went gamboling outside, so I
said yes, all right. I armed Ben and Grace against the cold with
snowsuits, fat jackets, mittens, hats, and boots, and they waddled
out ahead of me. The sky was clear and blue; the snow sparkled.
Herb slid onto the back of the toboggan, holding the rope. Then
came fearless Grace, snuggling up to her daddy, then me, then
Ben, my sweet little Ben. Herb's long legs were like iron rail-
ings along the row of his family, as one of our friends gave us
a little push. So fast – I hadn't known it would be so quick –
and the snow! I couldn't see, there was snow flying into my
face, I was blinded, out of control, clutching Ben, Grace against
my back – I was terrified, flying through space with Herb
bellowing, steering, and Grace screaming with joy, all of us
shrieking in the white screen of no picture, till at last we slid
onto the frozen lake at the bottom of the hill and slowly came
to a stop. We all rolled off the toboggan. Catching my breath,
on all fours, I looked up at Herb: his whole face was encrusted
with snow, his eyebrows like snowy mountain peaks; the furry
trim on the twins' hoods was white and glistening, their light
eyes peeking out of sugary faces. We all looked at one another
and laughed, we laughed so hard, turning in toward each other,

a circle of people who belonged to one another, and to no one else. That was the moment I felt us become a family, a unit apart from the world. That was when I became Pippa Lee.

Part Three

Part Three

Lion Turds and Potatoes

The night after her lunch with Moira, Pippa dreamed she was walking through a deserted shopping mall, chewing a wad of gum that had lost its flavor. The escalators were stock-still; rolling metal gates were clamped down over all the storefronts. She took the wad out of her mouth and started searching for a place to throw it away. She found the garbage, got rid of the gum, and was just wondering whether she could persuade someone to open the tobacco kiosk so she could buy some cigarettes when she heard a rough, breathy sound beside her. She turned and saw an enormous lion. He was serenely lapping up a puddle of strawberry ice cream from the floor. His mane was coarse and had golden hairs woven into the reddish thicket. Pippa was terrified.

The lion ignored her. He took a few bouncing steps and leapt gracefully into an enormous planter with an artificial palm tree stuck in it. Squatting, his back rounded, great haunches quivering, the lion shat onto the fake earth. He looked sheepish and vulnerable. Pippa felt sorry for the lion. Having accomplished his task, he sped off the huge flowerpot, as if disavowing his humiliation, and padded down an immobile escalator, moving as fluidly as a river, an invincible predator once again. Finding that she had a plastic bag conveniently wrapped around her hand, Pippa stepped over to the great turd and scooped it up dutifully, as she had a thousand times in Gramercy Park when walking Milo, their corgi, who'd died of pneumonia back in 1996.

'Mrs Lee?' She heard the voice coming from inside the tobacco kiosk. She walked over to the iron gate and peered inside.

'I would like some cigarettes,' she called out into the darkness.

'What kind?' said the voice.

'Those white ones,' she said.

Chris Nadeau stood behind the counter of the Marigold Village convenience store, watching Pippa, who was standing in her nightgown, holding a large baking potato that she had retrieved from the bin, a plastic produce bag over her hand, her gaze fixed somewhere behind his head. 'Marlboro Lights?' he asked helpfully. She didn't respond. He leaned over the counter and brushed her arm with his fingers. Pippa felt his touch as a shock from the metal gate of the tobacco kiosk, but it was enough to rend the dream. She looked down at her nightgown, the potato in the bag, her bare feet. As she looked up at Chris, his eyes filled with curiosity and concern, her mind gradually collected itself around her realization.

'Oh, my God,' she said softly.

'Would you like me to take you home?' Chris asked.

She nodded, handing him the potato.

By the time they got to her place, weak light was seeping into the darkness, like a drop of ink tinting a glass of water. One bird called out. Pippa made no move to get out of the truck.

'Mrs Lee,' he said. 'Pippa?' His gentleness surprised her. She felt tears on her cheeks.

'I'm sorry,' she said. 'This is the last thing you need. First your mother and now me.'

'It's not the same,' said Chris.

'It's just, I walk in my sleep. Recently, I have been. Something must be wrong . . . with me. The weirdest thing about this . . .'

'What?' he asked.

'I just feel so young,' she said. 'Like a very young person.'

'Well, you're young for around here,' he said.

'I don't mean that. When I was very young . . . I was always in the middle of some kind of drama . . . and as I got older and had a family, I gradually stopped being in the center, you know, I stepped aside, and other people were in the center; when you have kids that just sort of happens. And I got used to that. And now I am living this weird little drama and I am the protagonist and I just feel so crazy, even though I know it's a very common-place problem, millions of Americans are probably up buttering their stereos as we speak.'

He laughed, and so did she.

'You're an unusual person,' he said.

'No, I'm not,' she said. 'That's what I am trying to tell you. What's unusual is that I'm acting weird.'

'Trust me,' he said.

'Maybe you shouldn't tell anyone . . . about this,' she said.

'Okay,' he said.

She looked over at him and noticed his eyes for the first time. Dark as the bottom of a lake, they shone with the helpless honesty of a dog's eyes.

'Well, thank you – and good night,' she said, getting out and pushing the heavy door shut.

Herb was asleep. Stark naked, legs twisted in the sheets, his arms flung out on either side of him, his hairy barrel chest exposed, he looked like he had been washed ashore, like Odysseus on Circe's isle. But for Herb, the adventure was over, Pippa thought sadly. She wished that the future wasn't so predictable, that this house was not the death house. That it wasn't just a matter of time before he had the morphine IV in, and the nurse sat in the corner reading her magazine. Eighty years old. How long did he have?

Herb opened his eyes and saw her crouching beside him. 'What are you crying for?' He sounded irritated. He knew what she was thinking. He rolled over and went to sleep. She knew he was right. She had to stop being so sentimental. She needed a doctor, too. Pills, probably. She hated the idea, she never even took an aspirin if she could help it, but she was driving in her sleep, for goodness' sake. At breakfast she would tell Herb. She would tell him and he would fix it, say something dry and logical, and then she would do what he said. She didn't feel like sleeping, so she took a shower, dressed, and made coffee.

Finally, at nine o'clock, Herb came out looking sullen. He took a sip of the coffee and made a face. 'This is piss,' he said. Wordlessly she got up, took his cup, poured it out, and ground a new batch of beans. He sat there stewing. When she presented the second cup to him, he tasted it and said, 'Let's get a new machine.'

'This is a new machine.'

'Let's get one that makes a decent cup of coffee. We can afford it, we sold all our real estate.'

'I'll look them up,' she said. 'Maybe *Consumer Reports* –' Herb got up and went to the sofa, started reading the paper. She knew better than to try to talk to him when he was in a bad mood.

'Is there anything you want at the store?' she asked.

'No thanks.'

'See you at lunch then.' She walked out of the house and thought about what she wanted to buy. A beautiful melon, if she could find a ripe one. And prosciutto. She walked out into the driveway and stared at Herb's car, sitting there by itself. Where was her car? Had it been stolen? Seconds passed before she remembered it was parked outside the convenience store. Probably had the keys in it! She turned to go back into the house but stopped herself. Herb would flip about the car. He was grumpy enough already. How was she going to get to the convenience store? She could walk, but it was so hot – and Herb might pass her on the way to his office. She hurried around the house and looked across the pond. Chris's yellow truck was parked in the driveway. She wondered when his shift began. It wasn't even ten o'clock. What would she say to Dot? She started walking down the road to the Nadeau house. If Dot was there, she would pretend she was just stopping by, out on a walk. If she wasn't . . .

Pippa had reached the house. The toadstool cast a purple shadow on the grass. Dot's car was gone. Johnny spent every morning at the boatbuilding club – she remembered Dot mentioning that. Her belly tight with anxiety, Pippa rang the bell. Nothing stirred inside. She tried the door. Locked. She couldn't help laughing at herself as she crept around to the side of the house, to Chris's open window, and looked in. He was asleep. Pippa tapped on the window with her fingernail. He didn't move. She knocked on the glass. His head moved from side to side, as if to shake off the sound. Then he sat bolt upright and stared at the window.

'Chris,' she said. 'It's Pippa. I'm so sorry to disturb you.' He rubbed his eyes and swiveled around, putting his feet on the floor. He was wearing his 'What?' T-shirt, and held the sheet across his lap. 'I'll wait at the front door,' she said. She walked to the front door and waited. This was so embarrassing, it was beyond belief. He seemed to be taking a long time. Finally, she heard footsteps. The door opened. He was dressed, but he looked exhausted.

'I'm so sorry,' she said.

"S all right,' he said, his voice weak with sleep. 'Wassa matter?'

'My car,' she said. 'I left it at the store. I think the keys may be in it. I . . . have no way to get there and you're the only one . . .'

'Okay,' he said and walked out the door, toward his truck. She got in beside him.

'I shouldn't have done this. It's terrible, you won't get enough sleep.'

'Don't worry,' he said.

They drove to the convenience store. Her car was still there, with the keys in it.

'Oh, thank God,' she said. 'Thank you so much.'

'You want to get breakfast?' he asked, yawning. She realized that she was very hungry.

They went to the shingled Friendly's that was a part of Marigold Village. Pippa ordered bacon and eggs.

'This is a very strange moment in my life,' she said.

'You and me both,' he said.

'Yes?'

'Fired from a job I despise, I come home to find my wife on top of my best friend.'

'That's horrible,' said Pippa.

'The clichés were running fast and furious in Wendover, Utah, that Saturday night. But I've been thinking. Maybe there was a good reason for that layer cake of rejection.'

'Really? What?' said Pippa.

'I'm an asshole.'

Pippa let out a little laugh, then realized he was serious.

'I don't know why. I just always have been.'

'Hm,' she said.

'And what about you? Is there a reason you're potato shopping at two in the morning?'

'I don't know,' she said. 'I think maybe I'm ... Ever since we moved here ... I haven't felt right. I feel distanced from Herb and our life together, as if I were hovering above it, watching us. I wonder if it's to do with my age, and the fact that I – I don't quite know who I am these days, sometimes I'll be someplace and accidentally look in a mirror, and for a split second I think, Who's that middle-aged woman? And then, Oh, my God, it's me! It's an awful shock, I can tell you. But that doesn't explain why I've been sleepwalking.'

He didn't say anything, just stared at her. Pippa felt the blood creep up her neck, her cheeks. Her whole chest was getting blotchy.

'Maybe your brain is trying to tell you something.' His face was, as usual, expressionless. She could see the feathery lines of the tattooed Christ peeking out from the loose collar of his worn T-shirt.

'That tattoo you have must have hurt terribly,' she said.

'I can't remember.'

'My father was a minister,' she said.

He nodded, then ate for a time, looking down at his plate. Pippa watched him. His narrow face seemed very angular, almost wedge shaped, as though his cheeks had been chiseled away from his broken nose and chapped lips. One strong hand curled around his plate protectively.

'I tried to enter a seminary once,' he said.

'You were going to be a priest?'

'I wanted to, but – I wasn't their type.'

'Do you still have a vocation?'

'Just the tattoo.'

'You can have them removed.'

'You'd have to take my skin off. Anyway, it's a souvenir.'

'So you lost your faith?'

'I just stopped believing you could nail it all down.'

'I'm curious about you,' she said. And then she wondered if that was an inappropriate thing to say. He leaned back in his seat and looked at her, as if weighing something in his mind.

'Okay,' he said. And then he started to talk.

Chris

When Chris was sixteen, he tried to fix the dryer. He was a handy kid, always dismantling failing machines around the house, putting them back together so they hummed. It had gotten to the point where Dot didn't even bother with electricians. She just called in Chris. He had taken an evening course in appliance maintenance at the town hall, and this, coupled with his knack, gave her the utmost confidence in his ability to figure out why the dryer was howling like a cat in heat every time she turned it on.

Up to that point in his life, Chris had been good only at repairing machinery. Every afternoon after school, he would mope around the neighborhood, on the lookout for broken equipment. At night he drove around the sleeping streets with a group of high school miscreants, committing drive-by mailbox beheadings, or playing basketball in people's driveways until lights were flicked on and the cops were called. One summer evening, he and his crew went to the nearest movie theater, took stock of a local family out for the evening, returned to the family's home, broke in, raided the fridge, and cooked an entire barbecue in their backyard. In school, Chris stared listlessly at the teacher, his thumb worrying the eraser of his pencil, jerking it back and forth until, inevitably, it crumbled off.

On the day his mother asked him to fix the dryer, Chris had pushed the machine a few feet out from the wall and was lying behind it, curled up on his side, one leg bent, when he touched the wrong two wires together, went stiff, and started vibrating, 110 volts of electricity coursing through every cell of his body. Strangely, the boy was not afraid but awed by the power pulsing through him. A panicked Dot disengaged him from the current using a wooden broom handle. The medics arrived soon after. Chris was unconscious but alive. They had to work on him for five minutes that felt like fifty to Dot, who had her hands clamped to her face, terrified eyes staring out between spread fingers, during the whole proceeding.

When Chris woke up, his nose was filled with the smell of burnt hair and rubber; his mind was filled with God. For the first time in his life, he was on fire with ecstatic certainty: first of all, God was real as flesh. Second, the Son of God was neither meek nor mild. He was terrible as a tidal wave, merciless as a lightning bolt. He was the God of love but not mercy. His love was terrifying; it sounded like a million wings beating; it felt like being swept up by a tornado. And He reserved it for the renegades, the anarchists; those who wanted to bring the whole rotten structure of everyday human greed and insincerity to a trembling halt. Chris felt he had been chosen and warned. He started going to church daily and even brought home a woman and her two children whom he had found begging in the street, having missed the closing time of the local shelter.

Dot, who didn't even like her own family sitting on her best furniture, was horrified to find three shy, dusky strangers in her living room when she walked in, her arms gripping two bulging bags of groceries. But she couldn't exactly throw them out; the children were tiny. So she cooked them dinner in miffed silence, made them up two beds in the rec room, then took three aspirin and went to bed in tears, insisting that Johnny sleep with a revolver under his pillow.

Both Dot and Johnny were automaton Catholics; their practice was reserved for Easter and Christmas. The radical faith Chris displayed had no place in their home. His quiet, constant reading of the Bible worried and alienated them. An attempt at becoming a Jesuit novice – he offered himself to the order as a 'warrior of Christ' – had his parents mildly alarmed, then humiliated when his application was rejected after a psychiatric evaluation deemed him 'fervent to the point of irrationality.' (One lay Ignatian brother remarked, after Chris had left his requisite interview for the Vocations Panel, 'He would have been perfect for the Crusades.')

Once spurned by the Jesuits, Chris set about giving away as much of his parents' money as possible to the bums in Jersey City, twenties and fives filched from his mother's purse, his father's wallet. He started getting into bar brawls with hypocrites; he even got himself arrested once, for screaming '*Please stop lying to each other!*' up and down their quiet suburban street at two o'clock in the morning. He went straight from jail to a tattoo parlor and had the Lord bored into his skin for good. The boy was driving his mother crazy. His father felt completely impotent in the face of his son's problem. 'If it was drugs,' Johnny said, 'at least we could send him to rehab. But this . . .' He flapped his arms and let them slap his sides uselessly.

Chris left home soon after, in the Thunderbird his father had bought him for his eighteenth birthday in the hope that a vehicle would attract a girl (he sold the car a week later and gave most of the money away). His parents didn't try to find him when he left; they just sadly let him go. In the years that followed, Chris took a variety of jobs, as an electrician, mechanic, car wash attendant, all across the country. When he came to a new town, he would coast through it, searching for the poorest, most broken-down neighborhood he could find. Once there, he would seek out a rental apartment, or a room in someone's house. Occasionally, he lived in the back of his truck. Then he would find a church – be it Catholic, First Christian, Methodist, or Episcopal – pray there, help with whatever outreach programs they had going in the community, and then, after a few months or maybe a year, he would move on. Passing through Utah, he met and married a slight, bright-eyed Catholic girl. They prayed together frequently, made love seldom, barely spoke. Back home, his father, a meticulous dentist, was corroded with disappointment; his only son was an itinerant, a drifter, a religious fanatic. He kept hoping that one day Chris would come back to Jersey, finish school, find a profession. But no. The electrocution had happened nearly twenty years ago. Chris was a washout.

But Johnny and Dot didn't know the worst of it: over the years, Chris's belief in the Bible had sloughed away from him, like a scab from a healed wound. The God he still sensed with such acute certainty had somehow outgrown that good book; this was a deity too vast to be contained in a single system. There was no humility in thinking you had cracked the code. Chris stopped going to church, but he couldn't bring himself to tell his parents he had failed at being a Christian, on top of everything else. So he ricocheted around the country, his wife a stranger beside him, his faith now nameless, formless, dogging him, filling him with longing to see the Face that was veiled in darkness yet he knew was there. He was an exile, unable to stomach even the most innocuous corruption of everyday human life, to get a regular job, to settle into society, yet no longer enveloped in the golden light of dogma. He felt himself standing just outside a warm, safe, luminous circle – the circle of the Church. If only he could return to it. But it was too late: he didn't belong anywhere anymore.

Pippa listened to Chris's story, rapt. When he was done, he took a bite of toast.

'What are you thinking?' he asked.

'Nothing.'

'Tell me,' he said.

'I'm just thinking, you seem so bright, and it's a pity . . . that you never settled on a job you care about. It would make your life so much easier.' Why had she said that? So many thoughts – of worry, recognition, admiration – had darted through her mind as he spoke. But as usual, she said the one thing that made her sound like a materialistic housewife.

Chris sat back and looked at her. Surprise, hurt, and then anger appeared on his face in a sequence Pippa found disquieting. 'Okay,' he said. 'Well, thank you.'

'I didn't mean to offend you.'

'I suggest you go back to that little life you've puffed up for yourself. I'm sure you're very happy underneath all that misery.'

Pippa gathered her purse to her chest, slid out of the booth, her heart pounding in her ears. He was eating again.

'You're right, you know,' she said. 'You are an asshole.'

'Told you.' He hunkered down over the last of his home fries, waved his fork. 'See you in a few farts,' he said cheerfully, taking a bite.

She was already behind him and stopped, turning back, her jaw dropping. Then she walked to her car, trembling. But once she got in, she started laughing. She laughed so hard, she had to wipe tears from her eyes.

When she got home, she made spanakopita for Herb, folding neat packets of filo dough around a mixture of feta cheese and spinach. Then she settled into a reclining lawn chair on the patio, sipping a large glass of pomegranate juice. Herb was in his office. It was past one, he should be home soon. Pippa looked across the pond at Dot's house. The yellow truck was there. Then she saw the front door open. Chris walked out and got into his truck. He was the strangest person she had ever met. So unpleasant, yet so touching. The yellow truck pulled away just as Herb laid his hand on her shoulder. She turned, startled. 'Did you think I was a geriatric marauder?' he asked.

'I was just thinking,' she said.

'I'm sorry I was a grouch,' he said.

'It's okay.'

'It's so hot,' he said, 'I'm going to take a quick shower, and then we can have lunch.' She got up and put the spanakopita in the oven, tossed the salad she'd prepared. She served him out on the porch.

'Aren't you eating?'

'I had breakfast late,' she said. 'With ... remember Chris, that son of Dot's?'

197

'The half-baked one?'

'Yeah, I saw him outside the convenience store, and he asked me to breakfast.'

'That's weird,' he said.

'He told me he was an asshole.'

'Is he?'

'I think maybe he's just compulsively honest. Which makes him extremely unpleasant. Herb?'

'Hm?'

'I did it again.'

'What?'

'Walked in my sleep. I drove.'

'Oh, Jesus.'

'I woke up, and I was in the convenience store. Chris works the night shift there, that's how I know him, really.'

'I've never heard of driving in your sleep. How is that possible?'

'Maybe I'm an extreme case.'

'We better have you looked at.'

Dr Schultz saw only old people, it seemed to Pippa as she sat in his waiting room. If they weren't using walkers, they had white slacks on. Elastic waistbands, white tennis shoes, pastel tops. The very word *slacks* made Pippa cringe. Who passed a law that old people had to dress this way? Pippa glowered at them all. She was angry with them for living past their usefulness. For being so fucking slow. Old age repelled her; that was the truth of it. Herb wasn't old-old. Not yet. He was old, but his face was still basically on. He didn't have the gaping mouth, the glassy eyes, the imprecise movements of the truly aged. She was frightened of losing her husband to this joke of time. She knew she would love him and care for him, and gradually, depending on how long he lasted in his decrepitude, she would forget his strength, his invincibility, his irony even. Oh, God, it was awful. Pippa didn't want to live too long. Just long enough, she thought. Just

exactly long enough before she turned the final corner. The nurse
called her name.

Dr Schultz was a vigorous man. His bald head was shiny, the
whites of his eyes luminous. He looked like an athlete – a rower,
perhaps. The muscles in his powerful legs bulged under fitted
trousers. His feet were enormous. And he looked cheerful. Pippa
wondered how he kept that up, seeing so many revolting old
bodies every day. Maybe he was a sort of leech, she thought,
sucking his youth out of their age. He was asking her the usual
questions. Date of birth. What did your mother die of? Heart
stopped because. Because she took too much crank. No, leave
that out. Father? Aneurism. Any cancer in the family? Aunt Trish.
Poor old Aunt Trish. Pippa tossed her head. She was aware of
keeping a thought at bay. It hadn't entered the circle of her
consciousness yet, whatever it was, but she could tell it was
unpleasant. It cast a jagged shadow on her mind, caused her to
fidget and clear her throat, shake her head, anything to stop
herself from thinking – what? What was the matter?

'So. Mrs Lee. What can I do for you?'

Pippa started, realizing that she had drifted away as he watched
patiently. 'Oh,' she said, smiling. 'I – I have been walking in my
sleep.'

Dr Schultz wrote that onto his form, his big hand curled
awkwardly around a delicate silver pen. His handwriting looked
like crooked teeth, Pippa thought: tiny letters crammed up against
one another, slanted to the left. 'When did this start?'

'About a month ago.'

'What medications are you on?'

'None.'

'What about sleep aids?'

'Never. I don't take pills. I even take liquid vitamins.'

He looked up at her, surprised. 'Do you have a history of
sleepwalking?'

'A couple of times, when I was little. But this – I cook in my sleep. I smoke, which I don't, I mean I do a little now, but that's – I drove the car! To a convenience store. I was dreaming about being in a mall and there was a lion taking a crap in a flowerpot and I went to pick it up and it turned out to be a potato. At first we thought it was my husband, but then we set up a camera . . .' Her voice had risen; she was being voluble, humorous, as if telling a funny story at a party. She didn't know why she was acting like this. She felt breathless. '. . . and, surprise, surprise, it was me!'

The doctor looked at her, thinking. 'I'm not a sleep specialist, but some of my patients have problems with night mobility. Usually it has something to do with medication, or . . . dementia, which is clearly not the case here. Um . . . do you mind if I ask you a personal question?'

'No.'

'Is something upsetting you, or causing you stress?'

Tears came to her eyes instantly. Irritated, she wiped them away with her pinkie.

'I don't know.' An image of the beach, the day Gigi died: garnet flecks on her white dress, a flash of sky, then under bottle glass green water, swirling sand. She hadn't wanted to come back up.

'I can give you some medication which may keep you sleeping through the night. It doesn't always work. I mean, it's a sleeping pill. It depends on your tolerance.'

'Oh, God, I can't start taking pills.'

'You could grind them up in applesauce. Or put a lock on your bedroom door and have your husband hide the key.' Dr Schultz smiled wryly. 'I know it doesn't sound very scientific, but it would keep you inside. Listen, sleepwalking is not considered a psychological problem, it's neurological. But stress can play a part, especially in adult-onset cases. I'll give you a prescription. But it seems to me that you could benefit from a short period of psychotherapy. Just to . . . get your thoughts in order. You've made a big transition and . . . you seem like you have a lot on your mind.' She had her hand on the doorknob, was just about to turn it, when he asked: 'Do you have any hobbies?'

'Hobbies?'

'Yes. Anything you like to do – just for yourself.'

'Not really.'

'Hobbies can be helpful,' he said.

She thanked him and walked out the door, the image of his gleaming scalp and shiny eyes burned into her mind.

Pippa slapped her purse onto the coffee table. Herb looked up from his paper.

'He basically thinks I'm off my nut,' she said. 'He gave me a prescription for sleeping pills and the name of a psychiatrist.' She brandished the business card in the air. 'Notice it's not a therapist. That's because Dr Schultz thinks I'm going to need medication . . . and a locksmith.' She started giggling. 'He suggested we bolt the bedroom door from inside, and you hide the key. Oh, and I'm supposed to take up basket weaving.' She felt hysteria creeping up on her.

'You mean every time I have to get up and pee in the night I'm gonna be fumbling around looking for the goddamn key?' he said. 'Some doctor.' Herb looked at his wife. Two distinct red spots had appeared on her high-set cheeks, tears of laughter sparkled in her eyes. She seemed so alive.

'It's weird,' he said. 'Ever since we moved to the old folks' home, you look younger every day.'

She drove back to the mini-mall to pick up some photographs she'd had developed and buy fruit at Shaw's. They had some organic produce. Pippa was acutely aware of how poisonous the world was these days. Cell phones, cordless phones, computers, microwaves, vegetables, meat, carpeting – you name it, it was shedding some sort of toxicity. No wonder everyone was getting cancer. Pippa bought six ripe black plums and a big bunch of grapes. She collected her photos, then stood in line in the parking lot, outside the fish-monger's truck. The man drove all the way down from Maine every Thursday; she felt guilty if she didn't buy anything from him. Today she would buy a pound of clams, make spaghetti with clam sauce. Herb loved that. It was hot in the parking lot. She took the envelope with the photos in it from her purse and started flipping through the images: Herb reading, Herb eating cereal, views of the living room. Some pictures from a month ago, when Grace had come to see the place for the first time before going off to Kabul, her intelligent eyes red from the flash, hard mouth set.

'Hey.' Pippa looked up. Chris was standing beside her. 'Fish tonight?'

'I thought so,' she said. She was relieved to see him, surprised to be relieved.

'I'm sorry about the other day,' he said.

'Oh . . . that's all right.'

'I'm a jerk.'

'You're not so bad,' she said.

'How are you doing?'

'Oh, fine. Actually not so wonderful.' She felt emotion rising in her again, waved the packet of photos in front of her face to fan it away.

'I just bought some beer,' he said. 'Care to join me . . . after you get your fish?'

'I can make tomato sauce,' she said, waving her hand dismissively and abandoning her place.

They walked to the river. Chris's truck was parked there. He stopped at a small tree, almost entirely tented over with dense white webbing. 'Look,' he said, pointing. Pippa looked closely, saw caterpillars inching inside their translucent house, folding and stretching their black bodies. There were hundreds of them squirming around in there. It made her shiver. 'Tent caterpillars,' he said. 'They're all over the place. I've never seen this many. There's going to be an invasion of moths this year.' He climbed up onto the roof and held out his hand; she grabbed it and clambered up as well. They sat side by side and watched the river flow by, the current rippling the smooth, glossy water like muscle. Pippa was still clutching the photos in her hand.

'Who's that?' Chris asked, pointing to the photograph of Grace.

'My daughter,' said Pippa. 'She hates me.'

Chris didn't say anything. He took a sip of beer, and they both looked down at the river. The sun had moved, and the water looked metallic now, a band of pure silver-white, cutting through the trees. They stared until the light changed again, and the river reappeared. Pippa looked over at Chris. She felt strangely at ease with this person.

'I bet she doesn't,' he said.

'What?'

'Hate you.'

'It's just . . . she's angry at me all the time. I don't know why. I wish it was different. I miss her. I wonder . . .'

'What?'

'If I got it all wrong with her.'

It was getting dark. Pippa shivered. Chris took off his sweatshirt and put it around her shoulders.

'You're probably right about me,' he said. 'I probably should find a reasonable job. Something with a future.'

'It was a silly thing to say,' she said.

'No. It was . . . it was thoughtful. But. I'm beyond the pale.'

'So, what do you, I mean, you . . . drive around, take up residence in places, get a job, and . . .'

'I try to be of help.' He took a gulp of beer and shifted his weight. The metal of the roof let out a hollow thud as it buckled.

'What about here? Who are you helping here?'

He looked up at her, his thuggish, soulful face half-lit in the dying light, his deep-set eyes black holes. She felt her belly lurch, as though she had lost her footing and was falling.

'I'm leaving soon,' he said.

She had an impulse to grab his arm, but she sat still. 'Why?'

'I can't stay with my parents forever.'

'Where will you go?'

'Back out west, I guess. Or south.'

He jumped off the truck, helped her down, then walked her back to her car. She waved goodbye. He winked.

Every time she took her leave of him, he had to remind her that he was a crude waster. Yet she kept spilling her heart out to him. What the hell am I doing? she thought.

Back in the condo, she made the pasta. During the meal, Herb seemed to be lost in thought. He glared at his plate as if she wasn't there. She watched him, feeling awkward. She tried to remember how long it had been like this between them. Not always, no. They usually laughed so much. When had it gotten dried up like this? 'I joined Dot's pottery class,' she said.

'Good,' said Herb without looking up.

'Why do you think it's good?'

'Didn't that doctor think you needed a hobby?' A flash of dislike went through her. *Asshole*, she thought. Irritated, she got up and went into the bedroom, leaving Herb with the dishes. She wondered if she had ever done that before.

He walked in. 'Are you okay?'

'My mother used to lie on her bed like this with a plate of toast on her belly.'

'I know,' he said.

'I should take your blood pressure.'

He made an impatient gesture. 'It's fine. Okay then.' He made a sort of false exit, then stood there.

'I'll do the dishes later,' she said.

Backward

Pippa liked the feeling of the spinning, wet clay between her fingers, the way it rose up like a wave as she pinched it, the gray disk of the potter's wheel circling furiously between her knees. Transfixed by her power over the clay, Pippa let it grow too high, too thin. The pot listed, warped, then toppled and imploded, spiraling chaotically. It was her third class, and every effort had been a failure. The problem was, she wanted to make a vase with a long neck, not a stubby little potpourri container like everyone else in the class. She could tell her teacher, Mrs Mankevitz, a reptilian woman with a crooked back and bohemian taste in jewelry, disliked her for this. 'Mrs Lee?' she would say, 'Still unwilling to work your way up like the rest of us, I see.' On one such occasion, Pippa whispered to herself, as the teacher turned her hunched back to her, 'Oh, go fuck yourself.'

She hadn't meant to say it out loud, but Dot's head swiveled to look at her like a magpie spotting a rhinestone. Mrs Mankevitz halted, then turned slowly, long earrings tinkling, her toadlike face pale, her wide, lipless mouth set. 'What did you say to me?'

Pippa blushed. Fifty years old and still screwing up in the classroom.

'It's just that I don't care if I end up with a perfect pot,' Pippa explained. She felt the blood rushing to her cheeks, her throat tight. 'I don't need more clutter in my house. All I want is to feel the clay.'

'Well, if all you want to do is *play* with *clay*,' said Mrs Mankevitz, putting a veiny hand on one hip, 'I suggest you take a block of it home with you and knead it on the kitchen floor. This is a pottery class, not Montessori.'

Pippa looked around at the other members of the class. Six elderly women and a bearded old man, they all watched her complacently, curiously, as though chewing their cuds. Only Dot kept her eyes lowered, the coward. With a shock, Pippa realized she was being asked to leave. She felt sweat on her upper lip, her breath was shallow. She was trembling. She wiped her hands on a towel, took her jacket, her bag, and left.

Once in the parking lot, she couldn't face getting into her car. She didn't want to go home. She didn't know what to do with herself. It was eleven in the morning. Chris was asleep. Herb was in his office. She could go and see him. It was strange, Pippa felt, that she hadn't thought of Herb first. That was wrong. She must pay more attention to Herb. She walked over to the building where his office was, pushed open the door, ran up the flight of stairs to his door, knocked. She already had her first sentence formed: 'I got kicked out of pottery class.' There was a little laugh in it, the way she was saying it in her head; already she was making fun of Mrs Mankevitz, her gypsy jewelry, the way the whole class had stared at her as though she had just admitted to a sex crime. Herb would crack up about it. She could hear shuffling inside his office. She knocked again.

'Who is it?' Herb asked.

'It's me,' she called out. More shuffling. The door opened at last. Herb stood there, his clothes rumpled, his hair disheveled.

'Are you all right?' he asked.

'I got thrown out of pottery class,' she said. But it didn't come out funny at all. It came out pathetic. She sat down on the couch and saw there was a towel spread out on it, but she didn't really take it in.

'I told the teacher to fuck off,' she said.

'What did you do that for?' said Herb. His voice sounded so tired.

'She's a bitch, that's why,' said Pippa. 'What's this towel doing here?' There was a long silence. 'Were you eating and you didn't want to mess the couch up?' she asked helpfully.

206

'No.' He put his head in his hands.

'What?' There was a long silence then, it lasted a minute. Pippa's eyes traveled around the room until they came upon a pair of jeans. And there, threaded through the belt loops, was Moira Dulles's belt with the buckle, the silver star that she had admired. Pippa stood up, walked over to the bathroom door, and knocked. Then she tried the knob. The door swung open, and there was Moira, in Herb's teal blue V-neck sweater, sitting on the rim of the bathtub, clutching herself, her cheeks shiny with tears. She looked up at Pippa. 'Oh, Pippa . . . what have I done?'

Pippa stood on the threshold, staring stupidly at her friend, unable to collect her feelings. They ran higgledy-piggledy, like a flock of sheep scattering before an oncoming truck. Shock, anger, hurt, disbelief – they scrambled in all directions within her. She was unable to harness a single one of them. She felt Herb's hand on her shoulder. She shook it off, walked back into the office, and sat on the couch. He stood before her, frowning. Moira was sobbing loudly in the bathroom now.

'When did this start?' Pippa asked.

'Sometime after we moved here.' Herb sighed. 'I wanted it to just be an affair, Pippa, but it . . . isn't. I know it's horrible for you. I want you to have the money. You deserve everything.'

'Keep the money. You're going to marry her?'

'Oh, I don't know. At my age, it would be ridiculous. I just want to live, Pippa. It's my right. You've been burying me for the last few years. I feel the earth in my mouth. Almost like you're looking forward to it.'

'How can you say that?'

'You always said old age disgusts you. Why would I be an exception? I can feel you beginning to pity me, to be afraid of me. You're already in mourning. Be honest.'

'Yes, I am afraid of you getting old. Dying. It's normal to be afraid.'

'I don't want to be normal, and I don't want to be mourned.

I'm not a ghost. I want to live. No one knows when they are going to die. You could die tomorrow. I want to be alive. Fuck you for making me feel like an old man!'

'Herb,' she said in a flat tone, 'you *are* an old man.'

Herb sat down hard on the couch and looked out the window, as if lost in thought. Pippa watched him become a stranger before her eyes. The transformation was almost magical in its completeness. Next door, in the bathroom, Moira started baying like an animal. Then she went quiet. Pippa heard heavy breathing, a clatter, and a thump. Herb and Pippa rushed to see. Moira was lying on the floor of the bathroom, blood all over her arms.

*

'Killing yourself with a disposable razor. I don't think anyone's ever done that before,' said Pippa as she knelt on the bathroom floor, bandaging Moira's scraped up wrists. Moira, her face slippery with tears and snot, was sitting on the lid of the toilet, staring vacantly at the wall.

Herb stood awkwardly in the doorway. 'She was in despair,' he said. Pippa looked up at him sharply. He looked pale and clammy. 'She loves you, you know,' he added sheepishly.

'You should take a nap,' said Pippa drily. She still couldn't feel anything. It occurred to her that maybe she had actually stopped loving Herb without realizing it. No. That wasn't it. She remembered adoring him only this morning. Then why was she such a blank? Pippa had bought the first aid supplies only a week earlier, on impulse, to stock Herb's office bathroom. As she taped the bandages around Moira's wrists, something loosened from her mind and fell away, like a clump of earth from a crumbling dam. And all of a sudden, she was flooded with relief. It was her guilt that had fallen away, she realized, and landed right on Moira, smashed her to smithereens. Poor Moira. This was what guilt did to a person. Pippa felt time spinning back, back, back, until the bullet reversed out of Gigi's brain and she was innocent of murder, innocent of betrayal.

Pippa's luck had finally run out. She was the victim now. She had passed the guilt baton to Moira, and she felt so empty! Calm, peaceful, sad. Drained of her sin, Pippa felt herself slipping away, like a shade, no longer flesh and blood, no longer here, even. She stood up.

'That should do it,' she said. Then she took her handbag from the couch and walked out the door, down the stairs. Her steps made no sound. Herb didn't need her anymore. Nobody needed her anymore. Nobody at all!

Swerve

There was only one place to go. She drove over to the Nadeaus' house, cut her engine, and sat there. Chris's truck was on its own in the driveway. She went to his open window and looked in. He was sleeping. She dragged the ceramic toadstool to the house, stepped up on it, swung her leg over the sill, then squeezed herself through the window, but one foot got caught under the sash. She had to use her hands to dislodge her shoe, hopping to maintain her balance. Finally free, she turned and saw that Chris was watching her, smiling, his hands behind his head. 'Hi there,' he said.

Pippa lay down on the covers beside him. 'My husband is in love with a close friend of mine.' She looked over at his face. The broken nose, slack mouth, and the dark, dark eyes, burning with spirit or disturbance, it had to be one or the other, with eyes like that. She felt a shock of tenderness and desire. Suddenly they were kissing. His breath smelled pleasant, earthy, like a pond. There was a knock. Dot popped out of the wall, dressed entirely in white terry cloth, a big blond bunny. 'Are you okay?' she asked. 'I heard a sound . . .' Wide eyed, Dot looked down at them, shock and embarrassment spreading across her features.

'Hi, Dot,' said Pippa. She couldn't think of anything else to say.

Blond bunny bounced out. Pippa looked at Chris, a laugh in her throat.

'I better go talk to your mom.' Pippa smoothed her shirt and went into the kitchen.

'I didn't mean to upset you,' she said.

'Pippa. The man is thirty-five years old. You are . . . whatever you are. It's none of my beeswax.'

211

'I didn't think you were here.'

'My car is at the shop.' There were tears in her voice.

Chris was waiting outside for Pippa when she went to her car.

'I guess I'm going to pack,' she said.

Pippa drove back to her house. Herb's car was there. When she walked in, he was stirring Ovaltine into a glass of milk. He looked exhausted.

'I am so sorry it went like this,' he said.

'Me, too,' said Pippa. He walked up to her and put his arm around her. 'I'm sorry. I lost control of it. I – I care for you so much.'

'It's all so tired,' she said.

'What is?'

'This whole ... situation. We should just fast-forward to the divorce.'

She walked back into the bedroom and packed a few things. Why couldn't she feel anything yet? Most of her nice clothes were in storage, so she took a few pairs of jeans, her favorite boots. Shirts. What clothes do you need when you're thrown on the trash heap?

He tried to help her with her bag, but she ignored him, rushed it to her car. Once she got into the driver's seat, she realized she had forgotten her car keys. She smacked the steering wheel with a curse, then ran back into the house. The kitchen was empty now. She searched the room wildly for her keys. She had to get out before Herb walked back in. At last she saw them, chucked behind her morning coffee mug. When she drank that coffee, at eight that morning, she'd thought she was a happily married woman. As she snatched the keys off the kitchen counter, she glimpsed Herb's shoe on the linoleum. His foot was in it. She walked around the island of white Formica and saw him lying unconscious on the ground, a dark stain on his trousers where he had wet himself.

*

Herb was in the intensive care unit of the Ford Memorial Hospital, in a curtained-off room crowded with blinking machines, his mouth covered with an oxygen mask, a long, hollow plastic thread stuck into his wrist with a needle. Clear liquid dripped into the thread from a collapsed plastic bag hooked onto a metal stand. Ben stood at the end of the bed. He had driven up from New York. His eyes were wet behind round glasses.

'So I don't understand. You were in the car and you came back in, and he was on the ground?'

'That's right,' Pippa said, straining for the modulated tones of motherhood.

'Why did you come back in?'

'I forgot my keys.'

'Where were you going?'

'Ben, I don't really see how –'

'I'm just trying to get it all straight.'

'Does it matter if I was going shopping or to the hardware store or –'

'He just seemed really fine last time.' He was weeping. Pippa put her arms around her boy. Dear Ben. When she thought of Grace, on her way from the airport, her stomach tightened. But it had to happen. Grace had to say goodbye to her daddy.

Dr Franken came in. Only a few years older than Ben, with a round face and a slight lisp, this was the doctor they sent in to sympathize with the patients and their families, to try to stem their confusion. He had come in several times now to explain, first to Pippa, then to Ben, and to both again, that Herb had suffered a massive stroke, his brain was submerged in blood, he was living on the oxygen being pumped into him, it was the family's choice as to how long he should remain in that state and when he should be released into the stratosphere. But this time, Dr Franken had a different message to convey.

'Ms Moira Dulles – I believe she is a friend of yours, or of the family?'

'Of my husband,' said Pippa.

'She's a friend of yours,' Ben said.

'Not anymore,' said Pippa.

'Well,' said Dr Franken. 'She's a patient here, she was admitted with chest pains a few hours ago –' Pippa just about stifled a laugh.

The doctor looked up.

'Sorry,' she said. 'Go on.'

'I think she got a call, or someone told her, about your husband's stroke.'

'Mmm-hmm.'

'She wants to visit Mr Lee. She wants to visit your husband. Now. I actually saw her today, because I am a cardiologist. She is ... extremely distraught. I am sorry to bother you with this, but I had to ask.'

'She can come in for five minutes,' said Pippa.

Moira walked in and tossed herself on Herb's bed like a sack of sour laundry. Ben looked at Pippa, perplexed. Pippa rolled her eyes.

Later, in the visitors' lounge, she found herself fetching a cup of sweet tea for Moira, who, in her hospital gown, wrists bandaged, looked like she was fit for a lunatic asylum.

'Oh, Pippa,' she said, taking the steaming cup of tea. 'It's like the gods are punishing me.'

'Stop being such an egomaniac and drink your tea.'

'Please, please, please forgive me.'

'Forgive you for what?' asked Ben, sitting down in front of Moira.

'I ... I can't,' said Moira.

'Ben, your father and Moira were in love. That's why I was leaving.'

'*What?*'

'Oh, Pippa, I swear to God I will jump out a window if you don't forgive me. I was so stupid, so blind, so selfish, so –' Moira had gotten off her chair and was kneeling now. 'Please!' she said. People were staring at them over their newspapers.

'Okay. I forgive you. Get up,' hissed Pippa.

Moira got up and flung herself onto the nearest couch.

'You do not forgive her,' Ben said.

'You're right,' Pippa said. 'I don't.' She sat back and sighed. 'Why do I always end up with the crazy women?'

'How could Dad do that to you?'

'He was afraid of dying. He fell in love. It made him feel alive. I was . . . not altogether there at the end. I don't know.'

'Don't you even care?'

'How can I compete with *that*?' She waved her hand at Moira.

It was then that Grace appeared, far down the hallway. She ran toward them, looking young and frightened. Ben walked up to her, and they embraced. 'Where is he?' asked Grace, casting a curious eye on Moira.

As Ben led his sister into Herb's curtained room, a nurse whispered to Pippa that she had a phone call. She went to the high desk at the nurses' station.

'Oh, Pippa.' It was Sam.

'Hi, Sam.'

'I don't know what to say.'

'How much do you know?'

'Herb had a stroke. He was having an affair with Moira. She called and told me the whole thing this afternoon. Of all people, you are the last one this should be happening to.'

'Thanks, I guess.'

'I just want you to know that I love you.'

'I love you, too, Sam.'

'I mean, really.'

She sucked in her breath. So strange to hear him say it out loud. Exhaling, she said: 'Oh, Sam . . .'

'I'll come to see you later.'

'Okay.' There was a pause. Through it, Pippa saw her life with

Sam skidding toward her inevitably, like a runaway sled: the intimate outdoor wedding, a violet halo of flowers balanced on her head. In Sam's big, country kitchen, Pippa bending down to heave a large leg of lamb out of a steaming oven while Sam paced in his study. The artist's wife at last. It felt like something soft and heavy had been laid on her chest. A large bag of sand, perhaps.

'Sam?' she said quickly.

'Yes?'

'I don't want to make butterflied lamb ... anymore.' There was a silence. 'Do you understand what I mean?'

*

Hours later, Pippa and Grace got into Pippa's car. There wasn't room for all three of them to stay overnight in the room with Herb, and Ben wanted to be the one. The idea was to have a few hours' rest, then return to the hospital.

'Why did Ben get to stay?' asked Grace.

'I don't know,' said Pippa. 'He seemed to want it the most.'

'Oh, really?' asked Grace. 'How did you measure that, exactly? Do you have some sort of love-o-meter?'

'We'll rest for a few hours, and then we can –'

'Who's been smoking in this car?' asked Grace, a suspicious look on her face.

'I don't know,' said Pippa vaguely, feeling as though she'd been caught.

'Yuck.' They drove in silence for a while. Then, in a whisper, 'Was it Daddy?'

'No, no ...'

'If he started smoking again, maybe that's why he ...' She folded in on herself, knees drawn up to her chest. 'So his brain's just dead, just completely dead?'

'That's what they're saying, honey.'

They arrived at the house. Pippa opened the car trunk and took out the bag she'd packed that morning. A moth fluttered by

216

Pippa's face as she walked to the front door. It made her think of those sticky white tents, like cotton candy with worms in it. The larvae must have popped. Pippa remembered Chris. She missed him.

'Good night,' Grace muttered the moment they walked into the house. She walked down the hall, to Herb's study, and shut the door without looking back.

In her room, Pippa pulled on a pair of sweatpants and a T-shirt. It was better to be dressed in case she needed to go straight back to the hospital, she thought. Then she lay down in the bed. The fine cotton sheets felt noxious to her now. She thought of all the lying that had gone on in this bed in the past weeks. Why had he bothered to lie? She got out of the bed, sat in the small armchair in the corner, and lit a cigarette. She heard a soft knock and looked up. It was Grace.

'My God, you *are* smoking.'

'I'll stop soon.'

'But I've never seen you smoke in my life,' said Grace, coming into the room and sitting on the bed.

'I know,' said Pippa. She took another drag and inhaled defiantly, then stood up, took one of the decorative plates off the wall, and stubbed the cigarette out on it. Grace looked at her mother as though she'd gone insane. Pippa shrugged and sat in the chair again, her legs folded beneath her. For once, she wasn't afraid of Grace's disapproval. She felt she'd been dismissed, and was remaining in the family as a consultant. No, of course. Motherhood is forever. But what about if your child can't stand the sight of you? Do you just linger on, simpering, hoping for a change of attitude?

Grace sniffed. She was weeping. Pippa walked over to her and sat beside her. To her surprise, Grace leaned in to her, buried her head in her chest, and sobbed. Pippa stroked her daughter's head. 'I'm so sorry this had to happen to you,' she said.

'That's not why I'm crying,' said Grace. 'I'm crying because

I'm mean to you all the time, and I hate it. I don't want to be, I really don't.'

Astonished, Pippa took her girl's face in her hands, kissed her cheeks. 'I love you so much,' Pippa said. Poor girl, she didn't know what sickness had been passed to her through the women in her family. Mother to daughter in a line as long as Pippa had lived, and maybe further, maybe past Grandma Sally, to Sally's mother, and her mother before her; the chain of misunderstandings and adjustments, each daughter trying to make up for her mother's lacks and getting it wrong the opposite way. Some families were cursed like that. 'There is so much,' said Pippa, 'I wish I could tell you, but . . . I really don't know how.'

Grace put her finger to her mother's lips. 'Not yet,' she said. 'I just want to be your friend, Mom, while we still have time.'

'I would be honored to be your friend,' said Pippa.

'Not honored,' said Grace. 'Just happy.'

'Okay. Just happy.'

'Can I sleep with you?' Grace asked. Pippa felt a wave of almost excruciating happiness flush through her. She felt dizzy with it. 'Of course, sweetheart.' Pippa lay beside her daughter as Grace's eyes closed, her breathing deepened. Grace had wept in her arms. Imagine! The unfamiliar certainty of her daughter's love filled her with ecstatic disbelief. An hour passed. Pippa wasn't tired. She felt she should go back to the hospital. She would wait another hour. They would call if anything changed. She gazed at Grace, her young face so intent, even in sleep. Her brave little girl. She hoped there was still time to mend things between them. She heard a car pass by the house. Then it backed up, and white light swept through the bedroom. She looked out the window to see who it was. It was Chris. She switched off the bedroom light, walked into the kitchen, and opened the door. He was already standing there.

'I saw your light on, I wanted to see if you needed anything. My mother has a friend who works in the ICU; that's how we found out.'

'My son is with him. The idea is I'm supposed to be sleeping, but I can't.'

'I could drive you around a little bit.'

'Don't you have to work?'

'I'm off till five.'

'Maybe just for half an hour.' She went into the house, tiptoed down the hall, and peeked into her bedroom. Grace was asleep, huddled under the duvet. Pippa wrote a note, propped it up on the bedside table beside Grace, took her cell phone out of her handbag, drew her sweatshirt off the back of a kitchen chair, and walked outside. Chris was already in the driver's seat.

They drove around Marigold Village for a while. Pippa called the hospital to check on Herb, made sure they knew to call her cell. Then she looked out the window and stared at the wooden houses with their slanted roofs, the American flags drooping sleepily, as if resting for the night. 'I can't believe I ever lived here,' Pippa said.

'It's a weird place all right,' said Chris. He drove her past the convenience store, through the mini-mall parking lot where the fish man parked, to the river. He turned the engine off but left the headlights on; immediately, hundreds of white moths were whirling inside the columns of illuminated air, their wings flapping desperately, as if feeding on the light.

'They hatched,' said Pippa. They sat like that for a long moment, looking out at the moths.

'You said your father was a minister,' said Chris. 'Did he ever pray with you?'

'No. I went to his church every Sunday. But he wasn't praying with me.'

'Do you . . . anymore?'

'Yes. I don't know if I believe in anything, but I still pray. It's sort of automatic.'

'What do you pray for?'

'To be good.' She laughed. 'It sounds so childish when I say it out loud.'

'It's the only thing to pray for. The rest is wish lists.' There was something about him – so hard to put into thoughts – something genuine and transparent that she had only seen in children.

'Come on,' he said. He reached over her to pull open the latch of her door, then pushed the door ajar. His arm brushed the tops of her thighs. She got out. He came around to her side, took her hand, and led her to the back of the truck. There was a little door there. He opened it and drew her inside the orange shell. A match flared. He was lighting a candle. She could see now that there were several candles fixed on saucers along the wall and windowsills of the low plastic dome. He lit them, one by one. She shut the door so the candles wouldn't go out. The floor was covered in brown plush carpeting. A thin mattress was rolled up neatly and made a tidy couch. He patted it. Pippa sat down on the mattress ticking. He knelt in front of her.

'Do you want to pray for your husband?'

She felt irony pressing in on her.

'It's hopeless. His brain is dead.'

'Not for his brain. For his soul.'

'Oh. I don't know how to do that.'

'I don't, either,' he said. 'Let's try.' Chris took off his shirt. She had forgotten his tattoo. Jesus was in the room with them now. His fierce black eyes burned out of Chris's chest; his intricately drawn wings arched up over Chris's shoulders. Chris closed his eyes, clasped his hands, and looked at the ground. Pippa stared at the image on her friend's chest, and it stared back at her, unblinking, all seeing, awesome. This was not any Christ she had known. This was elemental, crushing divinity. She felt as though this truck was standing at the edge of space; she could not imagine anything beyond this moment, so foreign and yet so familiar, repellent and irresistible.

At last, Chris looked up at her, his face above the other face. He moved toward her. With deliberate, calm movements, he guided her off the rolled up mattress, pushed it so it flopped flat. She crawled over to him. She lay down. As he kissed her, she felt her mind fill up with him and nothing else. Candles glimmered behind his head. His hands were very warm. Her eyelids were heavy. There was a slowness in her now, a torpor, like a drug in her veins. She was slipping further and further into the moment until she felt herself at its very pit, where there were no images, only one color, only red, behind her closed eyes. She felt his hand on her sex. She opened her eyes. The tattoo loomed over her; the wings of the Christ seemed to spread wide and real above her, pulsing up and down, making the sound of two dry hands rubbing against each other as they brushed the sides of the plastic shell. This can't be real, she thought. And then, out of nowhere, a pleasure ballooned from her sex, swelled to fill her body until it burst, the sensation running down her legs, and she cried out, her head falling lifeless on the mattress, her body lank as the neck of a dead swan. Sadness trailed behind the pleasure like the tail of a comet. Grief and rage shot out of her mouth like flames. He held her head between his palms as she sobbed.

*

She did not know how she had gotten to the other side of the shell. She was zipping up her sweatshirt. 'I have to go back to the hospital,' she said.

She said nothing on the drive; words seemed distant as the stars. She didn't dare look at him, now that he had regained his human form. When they arrived at the hospital, she ran out of the truck; the glass doors slid open to let her in, then glided shut behind her.

Herb was breathing deep, difficult breaths, the plastic elephant's trunk strapped to his face, eyes closed. Ben was sleeping, curled up on the narrow cot by the window. Pippa shook him awake. Clutching the pillow, he jerked his head up to check his father. 'It's okay,' Pippa said. 'It's just time now. Go call your sister.' Ben pulled on his jeans, his shirt, and padded out into the hall in his socks. Then he turned. 'I'll go get her.'

Rebecca Miller

'She can take my car,' said Pippa.
'How did you get here?'
'Just call her, sweetheart.'
He walked off.
Pippa sat with Herb for a moment. 'I love you anyway, you know. I'll always love you, you bastard.' She stroked his head. Husband. Always and forever.
Ben came back in the room. He sat on the other side of Herb's bed, and they each held one of his big hands until Grace came in. She was already crying. She knelt and put her face on her father's arm.
A figure opened the curtain, a stocky lady with teddy bears printed all over her nurse's smock. 'Are you ready now?' she asked gently. Pippa nodded. The children were keening. The nurse removed the oxygen mask from Herb's face. His lips were blue. He took in a long breath, his chest straining. Another breath. His eyes snapped open, seeing something distinct, it seemed, just ahead. He began breathing hard, terrible breaths, as if he was in a battle, as if it was very difficult to die. His hand pawed the drip in his arm. He wanted it out. He wanted his dignity, Pippa knew. He wanted to go out whole.
'Can the drip . . . come out?' Pippa asked. The nurse gingerly eased the needle from Herb's arm, leaned in very close to his face, looked into his eyes. He focused on her, expectant. She held his arms and said firmly, 'It's okay.' Pippa squeezed his hand. The nurse moved to the corner of the room. A long moment of quiet. Then, finally, one long, gushing exhalation, as if a great animal were breathing his last. The nurse set the stethoscope on his chest for a moment. 'He's gone,' she said. 'I'm sorry.' Then she slipped past the curtain. Ben and Grace came to Pippa and held her and wept. She kept her eyes on Herb's face. It was already changing, becoming sharper, meaningless, a mask.
Chris was waiting outside the hospital when they walked out, after Herb had been taken away to the crematorium, and the

papers had been signed. He was standing by his truck. Pippa halted, seeing him, and Ben looked at him curiously. Then she got into her son's car, deeply embarrassed by what had happened in the truck. A fifty-year-old woman, fooling around in a pickup truck with the strangely spiritual, feckless son of her neighbor in the old folks' home! How Herb would have laughed. The whole thing was grotesque. She wished she could erase it.

'Stephanie and I want you to come stay with us,' Ben said.

'Hm?'

'We want you to live with us, Mom, Stephie and I. For as long as you want. We're going to take care of you.'

'Oh. Thanks, honey,' she said vaguely, imagining the clouds of cat hair that would rise up as she opened the foldout couch in their study, made ready to lie down. There you go. Yes. She would pack up their things as fast as possible, she would sell that death trap of a house, and she would stay with Ben and Stephanie, find a little place near them. Wait to be a grandmother.

Hopper

That night, Pippa dreamed she was driving into a dense cloud of white moths, thousands of them beating their wings against the windshield. Then she woke up, and she was driving inside a cloud of white moths. She felt blinded, claustrophobic. She stopped the car. But how would she get out? What if she was in the middle of the road? Someone would crash into her. She crept along, panicking, disoriented, trying to see the edges of the road so she could figure out where she was. She wondered if this could possibly be real. Had she had gone insane? Was she dreaming? Or maybe she was dead.

At last the creatures were thinning out. She could see through the fluttering wings, into the night. She was driving along her own narrow road, toward the intersection. She could see the convenience store across the road. It glowed with the cool blue light of a Hopper painting. So that's where she'd been headed. She tapped the gas pedal, rolled the car across the road tentatively, pulled in, and parked. She could see Chris inside. He was alone, leaning back, arms crossed, staring out the window, his skin stark white under the fluorescent light. She looked down at what she was wearing. Sweats and a T-shirt. Thank God, no nightgown. She got out of the car. The sound of tree frogs outside was shrill, continuous. She walked up to the store, swung the glass door open. As he saw her, his eyes followed her, but he didn't move, his expression didn't change. She walked up to the counter. They looked at each other. 'I'm awake,' she said.

Part Four

Yellow

Pippa stood at the threshold of the door to the bedroom and watched the children down the hall in the kitchen. They were sitting across from each other on stools, elbows on the counter, speaking softly, so as not to wake her. Grace was weeping, shaking her head. Ben was talking, looking out the window. He was telling her about Moira, Pippa was sure of it. To think they had once been inside her, those two people. She picked up the canvas bag at her feet and walked down the hall. She couldn't remember when she had packed such a light bag. Ben and Grace looked up at her.

'Hi, Mommy,' Grace said softly.

'Hello, my darling,' Pippa said.

'What's the bag for?' Ben asked.

'I'm going on a little trip,' Pippa said.

'A trip?'

'Yes I – I was wondering if you would mind – just go through the house and take whatever you want, then call these movers here.' She took a card from a drawer. 'They'll pack up the rest and take it to Goodwill.' The kids were watching her carefully. 'I left a check for them on the desk in my room. I don't want any of it,' she said.

'What about the memorial service?' Ben asked. Pippa hooked the Rolodex with her index finger and let it swing there. 'Pick a date and invite everyone on here. Except for Moira. Or invite Moira. What the hell.'

'Mom. You're actually leaving right now?' Ben was looking at her with a mix of disbelief and concern.

'Sweetheart. Your father was about to run off with a woman

229

I cooked for practically every other night over the past four years. I gave her advice on her love life, listened to her endless, egomaniacal complaining until I thought my head would explode, and then it turns out she's crying about my husband. I am not organizing his memorial service. I mean, I'll come to it. I'm just not buying the flowers.' Righteous outrage felt exhilarating and unfamiliar. Pippa took a breath and saw that Grace was staring at her with a trace of a smile, something dawning. Could it be – admiration? Just then, Chris's truck drove up.

Ben stood and went to the window. 'Who *is* that guy?' he asked, turning.

'My friend,' Pippa said.

'Your *friend*? What is going on here?'

'I'm sort of . . . hitching a ride,' Pippa said.

Ben put his head in his hands.

'I'm not driving off into the sunset, sweetheart,' Pippa said. 'I'm just . . . seeing what happens next.'

'I don't believe this,' Ben said.

Grace turned to him. 'She gave us half her life,' she said. 'Don't you think she deserves a vacation?'

*

Filtered through the dusty glass, the landscape looks smeared and faint, like a yellowing photograph. I roll my window down and watch the picture go vivid: flat, sandy land the color of rust; great, hulking slabs of brick red cliffs against the deep blue sky. I am skimming over pure planet, cut loose again. I glance over at him staring ahead into the clear distance as he drives. I feel as though he is driving me across a bridge of rock and sand. I don't know what is on the other side. I see little towns along the way. As I pass each one, I wonder, Could I live here? I try to imagine my other life, the one I left, but it is evaporating from my mind. I can remember images – Herb, the house in Marigold Village, my favorite vegetable knife –

but they are bloodless and unreal. I will go back, of course. Ben, Grace, the memorial service. But I feel an unfamiliar story unfurling in me. I have no idea how it will go, I don't know who I will be in it. I am filled with fear and happiness.

Acknowledgements

Thanks to my editor, Jonathan Galassi, for his subtlety and intuition; to my first readers: Cindy Tolan, Julia Bolus, Barbara Browning, Michael Blake, and Honor Moore, for their honesty and time; to my stalwart friend and agent, Sarah Chalfant; to David Turnley for lending me his experience; to Jane and Tom Doyle for getting lost with me; to Robert Miller for his memories; to the Jesuit Brothers of New Jersey for their kind help; to the Galway Literary Festival for giving me a chance to present the unfinished manuscript to an audience; to Claire Hardin, Kate Brady, Charissa Shearer, Emma Wilkinson, and Angela Trento for helping me with the kids; to Ronan and Cashel and Gabriel for the lines, and all they've taught me, and their love; to my beloved mother and father.

CANON‖GATE.tv

CHANNELLING GREAT CONTENT

WATCH

INTERVIEWS, TRAILERS, ANIMATIONS, READINGS, GIGS

LISTEN

AUDIO BOOKS, PODCASTS, MUSIC, PLAYLISTS

READ

CHAPTERS, EXCERPTS, SNEAK PEEKS, RECOMMENDATIONS

DISCOVER

BLOGS, EVENTS, NEWS, CREATIVE PARTNERS

SHOP

LIMITED EDITIONS, BUNDLES, SECRET SALES